WAHIDA CLARK PRESENTS

Karma 3:

Beast of Burden

Tash Hawthorne

Wahida Clark Presents Publishing
60 Evergreen Place
Suite 904A
East Orange, New Jersey 07018
1(866)-910-6920
www.wclarkpublishing.com

Library of Congress Cataloging-In-Publication Data:
Tash Hawthorne
Karma 3: Beast of Burden
ISBN 13-digit 978-1-9477322-6-1 (paper)
ISBN 13-digit 978-1-9477322-8-5 (ebook)

Library of Congress Catalog Number 2018906370
1. Urban, Contemporary, Women, African-American, Cuban-American – Fiction

Cover design and layout by Nuance Art, LLC
Book design by NuanceArt@aCreativeNuance.com
Edited by Linda Wilson
Proofreader Rosalind Hamilton

Printed in USA

Karma 3:

Beast of Burden

FOR XAVIER AND EVAN

ACKNOWLEDGMENTS

"Some say we are responsible for those we love.
Others know we are responsible for those who love us. "

-Nikki Giovanni

I'd first like to thank my Lord and Savior for His amazing grace and mercy. Thank YOU for never taking your hand off me.

To my family...your love, support, wisdom, encouragement, and belief has sustained me through my greatest of storms. Thank you for BEING.

To my students, my PHS Players (Adriana, Ayyaan, Jhaneyja, Johara, Jonathan O. Jonathan P., Kaleea, Kenia, Noah, Raiem, Tashanae, Valerie and Yakiem), your daily presence, thoughts, antics...energy has breathed life back into my spirit. Thank you for confirming my purpose; saving my life.

Lastly, I outstretch my sincerest appreciation to Ms. Wahida Clark and the entire WCP family for their faith, support, warmth, guidance, patience, and trust in me. The road has been long and tiresome, but we made it to this place AGAIN...this moment of accomplishment TOGETHER.

KARMA 3: BEAST OF BURDEN

Prologue

A "News at Noon" logo zooms across the screen with the ABC7 logo, current time and date set in the bottom right corner.

"We're going to shift gears now," an Asian-American news anchor says. "Former Newark police officer Money Parks was released from prison Monday after serving sixteen years for the attempted murder of his infant son."

The news camera cuts to video footage of Money walking away from his former domicile and toward a waiting car.

"I'm eager to get reacquainted with my family and reconnect severed relationships . . . apologize for what I've put them through," the former officer said through his lawyer. "Start my life over with God being first and the center of everything I do."

The news camera cuts back to the Asian-American anchor.

"In 2008, a day after the child turned one-year-old, Parks shot his infant son in the back while he was sleeping. Parks pleaded volitional insanity, a defense of irresistible impulse, which asserts that the defendant, although able to distinguish right from wrong at the time of the act, suffers from a mental illness or defect that makes him or her incapable of controlling his or her actions. His lawyer said he has since been treated for his mental illness, gone through counseling, and taught Bible study. The shooting marked the start of a cascade of troubles for Parks, who was promptly suspended from his job as a decorated Newark police officer. He lost custody of his daughter from a previous relationship, his mother died five years after his conviction, and he was accused of assaulting a guard with a deadly weapon upon learning the news of his mother's death. The mother of the baby whom Parks shot, Olympic gold medalist, Karma Alonso-Walker could not be reached for comment."

An aged hand places a bottle of alcohol to its lips. The 46-inch television screen fades to black. A pair of brown eyes peer into the oversized black monitor. A chestnut brown reflection stares back. A white bottle of pills jiggles in another aged hand. Nostrils flare. Swollen fingers ball into fists.

Chapter 1

Karma heard the panic in her son's voice as he bellowed, "Mom!"

"Mekhi, what's the matter?" Karma asked.

"Mom! Papa said he can't breathe!" he uttered.

"What?" Karma struggled to hear her son over the loud music and video game sound effects in the background. "Mekhi! Turn the TV down!" She slid to the edge of her seat.

"He can't breathe! He's sweating and, and—"

"Call nine-one-one, Mekhi! I'll be right there!" she assured him, rising from her chair. Karma slammed the phone down, snatched her coat and purse off the coat rack, and ran out of the office.

"*Tio!*" she shouted, running through the dining hall toward the kitchen. "*Tio!*"

Miguel looked up from the prep station and stopped dicing an onion. He immediately noticed the alarm in his niece's voice. He retrieved a cloth from the pocket of his apron and cleaned his hands with it while meeting Karma at the service station.

"*Que pasa?*" he asked.

"Mekhi called. Something's wrong with my father," she informed him, zipping up her coat.

"Okay. Go, go," he insisted.

"*Le llamaré!*" she yelled over her shoulder as she raced out the door of her restaurant.

* * * * *

Lorenzo lay crumpled on the floor in the fetal position when she entered the house. She'd expected to see paramedics and Mekhi, but neither was in attendance. In that moment, Karma realized Mekhi hadn't called them at all. Her father's head was resting in a pool of vomit, his body seizing, and creating a steady knocking sound against the wooden floor beneath him. The sight before her stopped her breath momentarily. It was the second time she'd found one of her parents in a horrific state on the floor.

Not again, she thought. *No . . . no.* Karma snapped out of her entranced state and ran over to her father. "Mekhi?" she yelled. "Mekhi?" *Where is Mekhi?* Karma threw herself onto her knees, snatched her wool scarf from around her neck, and placed it under his head.

"Daddy? Daddy!" she screamed. "Please. Please, don't do this to me!" Karma frantically reached into her pea coat pocket and retrieved her cell phone. She dialed 911.

"Nine-one-one, what's your emergency?" a woman with a husky voice breathed through the line.

"I need an ambulance to come to 598 Elmwynd Drive in Orange, New Jersey. My father's having a seizure," Karma responded hysterically, as she wiped the sweat off

4

her father's face.

"Where is your father located, ma'am?" she asked calmly.

"He's on the floor in the living room. I'm with him," Karma replied, holding his face in her hands.

"How long has he been seizing?" the operator implied.

"I-I-I don't know. My son called me while I was at work. I-I just got here a couple of minutes ago." *Mekhi.* Karma's wild, honey-brown eyes scoured the room for her son. *Where is he?*

"Okay, ma'am. If he is not already on his side, carefully roll him onto—" she began.

"He's already on his side!" Karma stressed.

"Okay, good. Are his eyes rolled back into his head?"

Karma zoomed in on the windows to the soul of the man whom she loved and hated, feared and fought. His lids fluttered. The whites of his eyes were visible,; nothing more, nothing less.

"Yes!" Karma bellowed.

Suddenly, the rocking stopped. The room became silent. Lorenzo was still. Karma's untamed eyes widened, and she immediately searched her father's face for life. His eyes were still lost and his mouth-—-agape.

"Daddy? Daddy?" Karma cried. Tears flooded her eyes as the vision of her brutally beaten mother came into view, clouding the image of her father before her.

"Ma'am . . . Ma'am," the operator called.

"Daddy? Daddy?" She rolled him over onto his back.

"He's not breathing! Daddy?"

"He's stopped breathing?" the woman asked, innocently.

"He's not breathing!" Karma replied, hysterically .

Chapter 2

She's watching him suffer . . . watching him die, Karma thought. How brave the young black nurse with the sharp pixie cut was. To do such a job as taking care of a perfect stranger. Karma stood, arms folded across her chest with her back against the cold frame of the doorway to her father's hospital room. She watched the nurse take the empty bag of saline down from the intravenous infusion pole and replace it with a new, full one. She checked his vitals on the cardiac monitor, then made sure his IVs and heart monitor patches were in place and secure before leaving the room.

The crease between her brows grew deeper as she struggled to comprehend all that Lorenzo's doctor told her. The utterance of *"cirrhosis of the liver"* and *"chronic liver failure"* became a deafening echo in her ears, making it difficult to hear anything else. She winced as she closed her eyes and shook her head in disbelief.

The past sixteen years shared between father and daughter had been good ones. Lorenzo moved in immediately after Money's prison sentence. He'd become the very much-needed father-figure for Mekhi, going beyond what was asked and expected of him. Wherever

Lorenzo went, Mekhi was there at his side. He began to prepare him for manhood at the age of three, teaching him the necessities of surviving in the world as a black man. Mekhi knew how to tie a tie, change a tire and oil, how to ride a bike, fight, camp, swim, play chess, cook, and fish all before the age of ten. Sex education and shaving came later.

Lorenzo's approach was very much military, and often created rifts between him and Karma. She thought he was too hard on her son. Expected too much from him too early. And she swore the pressure would eventually cause the boy to have a breakdown. But Lorenzo always reassured her that his way was best and most effective. As much as Karma hated to admit it, her father's way was the ONLY way. Mekhi's room was always spotless, his clothes ironed to perfection, his hygiene and behavior beyond superior and grades in school, exceptional. He exceeded in any sport he explored, becoming a great threat to his competition; especially in swimming and his mother's pastime of track and field.

The soldier's alcohol dependency became non-existent once he moved in with Karma. His love for her and Mekhi was far greater than any taste he had from time to time. That, and he didn't want to hear Karma's mouth. He only drank during the holidays and even then, Karma gave him grief. He had it under control. That is, until the anniversaries of Soleil's death became too much for him to handle. The last one worse than the one before. All of them forcing him to remember. To face her absence every time Mekhi reached a milestone. He was supposed to experience those great moments with her. But she was gone. And he missed her. With each day that passed, his need for her became greater. He'd abandoned her, leaving her with another man who'd loved her to death. Lorenzo had it under control. He hid the bottles and cans in a place Karma never suspected: under the floorboards in Mekhi's closet. He had it under control . . . . or so he thought.

"How long does he have?" Karma asked in a trembled whisper.

Dr. Saddler pressed Lorenzo's chart against his chest and sighed. He'd been his patient for over twenty years. And in that time, the two had become very good friends. He'd forewarned his fishing buddy about this very day months ago. And Lorenzo, with a stern military nod and squared shoulders, told him he'd get a handle on it. The drinking.

"A couple of days. A week at the most," he replied, his eyes sad.

Karma exhaled a breath, a visibly tortured one. She wasn't ready to lose her father. Not like this, not so soon. There was still so much for him to do. She needed him. Mekhi needed him. *Mekhi*. Tears of rage filled Karma's eyes as she thought about her only child's desertion. He was a coward, something he'd never been in all his seventeen years on Earth. And that didn't sit well with her.

She looked over at the man whom she blamed for her mother's demise. He lay still, small in stature, buried beneath a mound of white sheets and blankets. His deep slumber was accompanied by beeping machines and voices outside his door. Their relationship over the years, mostly during her teenage and early adult years, had been tumultuous. His absence, constant. The other women, too many to count. But the death of her mother had brought them closer. Unfortunately, that wasn't the only thing her mother's passing shepherded. Alcoholism found its way into their lives, creeping in slowly and steadily. And staying without Karma's consent. She thought she was enough for him then-——-thought Mekhi was enough for him now. But as she studied the man whose appearance was not his own anymore, Karma knew this is what he'd wanted all along. To die. Not with dignity or honor. He just wanted to die. To be with his wife. To leave here in pain, as she did. Because after all, he hadn't been there to protect her. All the medals of honor and purple hearts, wars conquered overseas and at home couldn't and didn't change the fact that her father was no hero. Not a real one. Not by any means. Not in his eyes.

"I'm sorry, Karma. Truly, I am," Dr. Saddler continued.

Karma met the older man's eyes. They were heavy with grief. "I'm sure you tried to help him. I *know* you did. But I learned a long time ago, Dr. Saddler, that you can't help those who don't want to be helped." She sniffled. "My father's always been a stubborn man. He's always been a selfish man. If this is what he wanted . . .. . . so what's the next course of action?"

"Hospice. I'll need your permission—your written consent to transfer him to that unit where they'll make him as comfortable as possible," he replied.

"Oh, God!" Karma yelled, throwing her head back. She balled her hands into tight fists and pounded her thighs with them. "I can't!"

Dr. Saddler removed his glasses from his nose and wiped his hand over his aged face. There was nothing he could say or do to comfort her. So he just watched her come to terms with her new reality, with the inevitable.

"Goddamnit, Daddy!" Karma hollered into the room's stillness.

Chapter 3

"Mekhi!" A very worried and nervous Desiree exhaled as she swung open the door for her cousin. She wrapped her toned arms around his thick neck. "You okay? Where have you been?"

"Everywhere," he replied, shivering from the cold remnant of brisk October air. With his shoulders hunched, he removed his glove. Quickly, he moved past her, up the stairs, and into the warmth of their kitchen. Mekhi snatched his other glove off as Desi closed the door behind them. He proceeded to rub his massive hands together as she ascended the steps.

"Everybody's been trying to reach you for hours. Where's your phone?" Desi asked, studying the panic-stricken young man before her.

"I don't know. I lost it somewhere between here and Vauxhall," he admitted.

"Vauxhall? You rode all the way to Vauxhall, Mekhi?" Desi was shocked and watched him pace the freshly polished wooden floor.

"Yeah. Vauxhall, then to Springfield . . .. . . then Summit." Mekhi's answer seemed nonchalant.

Desi shook her head in astonishment. "My dad's out

12

looking for you now. And my mom——-"

"Is with mine at the hospital." He sniffled, completing her sentence.

Their mothers were still as close as sisters.

"Yeah." Desi smiled sadly. "Did you eat?"

"No. I'm not hungry."

"You have to eat something, *primo*," she urged. "Here." Desi handed him a banana.

"Thanks," Mekhi mumbled as he finally sat down on one of the bar stools at the island.

He peeled the skin off the ripened fruit slowly, then took a bite out of it. Mekhi raised his ocean blue eyes, meeting her emerald green gaze.

"They're going to be home soon," Desi said carefully.

"I know," Mekhi murmured. "I'll be gone before dey get back."

"They're going to ask if I've heard from you."

"I know." Mekhi cast his baby blues to the floor.

"What do you want me to tell 'em?"

"Tell 'em whateva you want." Mekhi shrugged, taking another bite of the fruit.

"*Primo*----" Desi began.

"What!" he snapped.

Desi, caught off guard by his curt response, folded her arms across her chest and frowned. "All I was going to say was, whatever happened this morning, I'm sure *Tia* will understand. Just be honest with her."

As much sincerity as there was behind her words, Desi knew just as well as Mekhi that it was the farthest thing from the truth. Mekhi gave her a knowing glance. "It wouldn't hurt to try," she continued softly.

"I gotta go," Mekhi muttered, his face stern and emotionless. He couldn't tell Desi, let alone his mother, why he'd left his grandfather to die. He knew his mother well enough to know that she probably thought his abandonment was done out of fear. In fact, he guaranteed it. But it wasn't. Something much greater got a hold of him just before his grandfather fell to the floor. Something Mekhi would be haunted by for the rest of his life.

Karma raced up Central Avenue with no regard for her life or that of Indigo's. Indigo rested one hand on the dashboard and the other on the passenger window as Karma dodged in and out of lanes.

"Karma!" Indigo screamed, as she darted from behind a slow-moving hoopty.

Too deep into her rage, Karma didn't hear her cousin's sporadic shrieks of terror, but kept her eyes forward. All she could think about was getting home to Mekhi. She was uncertain if he was there, but she figured if he wasn't, he'd get there eventually. She didn't care if she had to stay up all night waiting for him.

Karma made it as far as Central and South Munn before coming to a hard, screeching halt at a red light. She squeezed the steering wheel tightly as Indigo breathed a sigh of relief. Indigo looked over at her unsettled cousin and carefully placed her hand on her thigh.

"Karma," she said softly.

Instantly, Karma cut her eyes at her cousin's hand, then gazed back to the road ahead. She'd forgotten Indigo was in the car with her.

"Pull over after this light turns," Indigo insisted gently. "Let me drive. Please."

As Karma gripped the steering wheel tighter, she gave Indigo's offer some thought. The light finally turned green, and she did as she was asked. She put the car in park and allowed the purr of the engine to bring her down a notch.

"What am I gonna do without him?" she asked, her hands still holding firm to the steering wheel. "What am I gonna do with Mekhi after he's gone?" She slowly turned to look at Indigo.

Karma knew it was only a matter of time before Mekhi would lose himself and fall back into his routine of going in and out of juvenile hall. The Essex County Juvenile Detention Center had become her son's second home within the last two years . And there was no one else to blame but herself. Her father, growing old overnight it seemed, did what he could with the teen. But his strength was no match for Mekhi's when he fell into his fits of rage. Karma had been forced to call on Stuff for reinforcement on a number of occasions. And he proudly stepped in, tackling Mekhi's fury. Taking on the responsibility of physically putting him back in his place when necessary.

"You know Stuff and I are here for you, *prima*," Indigo

responded, soothingly. "And you also know Stuff will do anything you ask of him. Just say the word."

"Someone's gonna get hurt tonight," Karma admitted, with tears in her eyes.

"No. Don't say that," Indigo contended .

"They are, *prima*," Karma countered, unsympathetically. "I curse the day I opened my fuckin' legs to his father." A storm was brewing within her, and she wasn't confident about her or Mekhi's ability to weather it.

Mekhi sat on a plastic milk crate, replaying the day's events over and over again in his head. Going to Desi's had been a waste of time and a big mistake. He didn't know why he'd gone there in the first place. Probably because he had nowhere else to go and needed some source of comfort. Mekhi left just as quickly as he'd come.

Out of places to hide, Mekhi decided to make the journey home. He made a quick stop at the Hess gas station on Central Avenue to put air in his tire, and then went to the Burger King across the street. He'd grown tired and hungry over the course of the day, so he bought himself a tender-crisp chicken sandwich and fries to fill both voids. He cruised up the long driveway with the bag of food in hand, then hopped off his trusty two-wheeled steed before finally finding refuge in his clubhouse. His sacred place. A wooden shack held together by old, rusty nails. The worn, rotting walls and ceiling were covered with posters of expensive vehicles, classic mafia and black gangster movies, Tupac Shakur, Bob Marley, and nude women. His grandfather's card table with the missing fourth leg sat in the middle of the makeshift abode. A chessboard and its pieces sat atop it. Three built-in shelves held framed photos of his three best friends and him, stacks of magazines that served their individual interests, plastic unopened bottles of Gatorade, and playing cards. The door was an old sheet of heavy scrap metal. His place of solace wasn't much to look at it, but it served its purpose for Mekhi and his friends. He felt safest there. However, sitting there in the quiet of his cold, ragged domicile, Mekhi couldn't ignore the fear that had also taken residency in that modest space. He hoped he had more time. Time to gather his thoughts. Time to explain what happened. He hoped his mother decided to stay at the hospital for the remainder of the night. He hoped she'd be so overcome by exhaustion that she'd send someone else to the house to stay with him. But he knew his wishful thinking was just that. His mother was, most likely, beside herself. And she was coming for him whether he was ready for her or not. Mekhi's world was going to be rocked upon Karma's return.

"Mekhi?" Karma shouted, marching up the driveway into the backyard. "Mekhi?" Her face was hot and flushed, her heart pumping five times its normal rate. "Mekhi?" she hollered again as she approached the well-constructed dwelling.

Before Mekhi could take a bite out of his sandwich, Karma was throwing her body against the door, ripping it from it hinges. Mekhi, startled by his mother's violent intrusion, jumped at the sound of her body connecting with the metal door.

"What the fuck are you doin'?" Karma shouted as she ran up on the boy, taking his coat collar into her gloved hands. "Where were you!" Mekhi grabbed his mother's hands and struggled to keep a steady balance.

"Get off of me! Get off!" he ordered.

In response, Karma hit him with a double open-handed slap. He was going to get caught with a triple, but he grabbed her hand before it reached his face again.

Now at forty-two-years-old, Karma was tired. She'd left the world of track and field behind after solidifying her spot as the 'fastest woman in the world.' She'd set the fastest times in the 100 and 200-meter dashes at the 2012 Olympics in London. Then added the 400-meter dash to those successes at the 2016 Olympics in Rio. She retired on top, thereafter, just like she wanted. Her records withstanding today. Karma had traveled around the world and back again as the co-chair of the POTUS' Council on Physical Fitness and Sports. She continued her mother's selfless work in the city of Newark, feeding and clothing the homeless and housing victims of domestic violence at the crisis center she built in Orange, named after her mother. She and her uncle Miguel opened another Cuban restaurant in downtown Montclair, also named for her beloved mother. And she was currently in the process of opening a coffee house in South Orange's Village and Newark's Penn Station. Her exhaustion was well deserved.

Karma managed to snatch her hand out of Mekhi's grasp and struck him again with a closed fist. "How could you!" she exclaimed. "How could you?" she repeated, her five-foot-seven self, towering over a six-foot-four Mekhi. Mekhi did his best to cover his face, but the blows kept coming from every direction.

Pop! Pop!

Karma struck him in the nose and mouth, busting them wide open. Mekhi figured she'd be satisfied with that, but she grabbed him by his collar again and dragged him onto the floor.

"Ma!" Mekhi hollered, scurrying to his feet.

"You left him!" Karma cried, punching him in his head. "You . . .. . . I'll fuckin' kill you!"

"Do it then!" Mekhi sobbed, grappling with her. "Do it! I don't give a fuck!"

Karma stopped. Out of breath and stunned by his admission, her chest heaved as she focused on the spent man-child before her. Defeated, Mekhi scowled back at her. Hatred and ire lived behind his gaze. And because he was his father's son, she knew he would hit her back if she continued her tirade. Karma had seen that look only once before. It shook her then as it did now. Cringing at the thought, she bit her lip and balled her gloved hands into fists again. Her nose was running. She sniffled back a fresh set of tears and wiped her nose with her coat sleeve.

"Call your uncle . . . and tell him to come . . . and get you," Karma mustered in a quiver.

Mekhi locked his jaw as the stare-down with his mother

prolonged. Blood dripped from his nose and mouth profusely. One red river. His lips were swelling rapidly. With the back of his hand, he wiped away what he could of the hot, flowing liquid. He was more than happy to get away from her. He didn't care whether she wanted him gone for a day or a month. He just wanted to get as far away from her as possible. And so he did. With his lip curling in one corner, Mekhi gave his mother a final once-over before walking out of his haven.

Karma closed her eyes and shook her head in dismay. She was losing Mekhi.

Hell, who was she kidding? She'd lost him a long time ago. Two years ago, to be exact. And she didn't know how to get him back.

Indigo and Stuff arrived at Karma's house in under ten minutes. Since they all lived in Orange now and were only 2.2 miles apart, getting to each other's home was only a hop, skip, and a jump.

They peered out of their windows at the dejected young man who sat motionless in the gazebo, head bowed and his hands buried in his coat pockets.

"Aww, baby, look at his face." Indigo sighed.

"I see it. Sis did a numba on 'im," Stuff confirmed as he turned the ignition off.

The couple climbed out of their Barolo black Range Rover, closing their doors behind them.

"Mekhi, baby, are you all right ?" Indigo asked,

approaching him with caution. She took his face into her gloved hands and examined it, then gently brushed his bruises and cuts with her thumbs. Mekhi never acknowledged the concerned woman. Indigo turned and looked back at Stuff in despair.

"Go on in da house, babe," he began. "I got 'im."

"Okay," Indigo agreed hurriedly.

"Come on, man," Stuff urged the troubled boy as he grabbed the nape of his neck lovingly.

Mekhi rose from the wooden bench with great hesitation. He was having second thoughts about going with his aunt and uncle. His mother wasn't all right , and as furious as he was with her, he didn't want her to be alone. Even though they lived in the Seven Oaks section of the city, in which only those with money could truly call *home*, Mekhi knew crime traveled. And he just didn't want any evil greeting her at their doorstep.

As he walked to the car under the wing of his uncle, he thought about the stare-off that ensued between his mother and him. How her eyes looked like two burning infernos. She'd gone temporarily insane, and to be quite honest, Mekhi had feared for his life. And that of hers. He knew what she was capable of. He just didn't know that of himself.

Indigo stepped up to the door as the guys settled into the warmth of the luxury jeep. She placed her hand on the doorknob and attempted to turn it, but it wouldn't rotate. Karma had locked it.

"Oh, my God," Indigo whispered.

A number of rooms were lit, so she knew her irate cousin was still awake. She also knew Karma wouldn't dare go to sleep without seeing Mekhi off. She sifted through her oversized purse and cursed herself after realizing she left her keys to the house on her bed.

She pressed the brightly lit doorbell, then waited. Measured footsteps sounded behind the heavy wooden door. The clicking of locks ensued. Soon after, the door opened and Karma stood before her in a satin robe and gown. Her blonde, frosted mane loose and hanging down her back. Even with swollen eyes and the grimace on her face, Indigo thought her cousin was breathtaking. She'd aged well, despite the number of years of pain and suffering. They both had.

"You all right?" she asked sincerely. Karma rolled her eyes and walked away. Indigo entered the toasty abode, closing the door behind her. Her one and only cousin was stressed beyond measure. Karma settled behind the island in the kitchen, turned a burner on, and placed a kettle of water atop it.

"You want some tea?" she asked, exhausted.

"No, thank you." Indigo eyed her closely. "Uh, how long do you want us to keep him?"

"I don't know, and I really don't care," she replied, matter-of-factly.

"You don't mean that."

"I don't?" Karma challenged, her eyes cold and serious.

A loud silence settled between them. "He was scared, Karm," Indigo stressed.

"I know that, Indigo!" Karma snapped, slamming the island drawer closed. "I know that," she reiterated just above a whisper.

"Then go outside and tell him you love him. Tell him you're sorry for beating him."

"No."

"He needs you right now."

"No, what he needs is to stay the fuck away from my house until I'm ready for his return."

Sighing in defeat Indigo huffed, "Fine. Have it your way. I'll call you when we get home."

"Mm-hmm," Karma muttered.

Indigo cut her eyes at her cousin before making her way out the door.

Karma dropped her head and grabbed hold of the island's edge, holding on to it for dear life. Afraid that if she let go, her legs would give way beneath her, and she'd become one with the floor. So, she just held on . . . held on . . . and held on some more.

Chapter 4

"Ay, yo. Y'all comin' through tonight or what?" Curtis asked.

"Nigga, you know we are," Jamie replied with a smirk. "When have we eva missed a game?"

"Never," Curtis retorted.

Carmine and Jamie nodded in agreement.

At the intersection of Martin Luther King, Jr. Boulevard and Springfield Avenue, Mekhi stood at the bus stop waiting for the #44 bus. He stood among his three best friends in a crowd of other boys dressed in burgundy, white, and khaki.

"Exactly. So, why would we start now?" Jamie countered.

"You right." Curtis nodded with a smile. "My bad, man. I'm trippin'."

"Yeah, you are," Carmine replied. "What? You nervous, man?"

"A little," Curtis admitted, shifting his weight from one foot to the other.

"Why? Because they got Chad Holmes now?" Carmine continued.

Curtis raised his eyebrows in confirmation.

"Aww, man. He ain't shit," Carmine stated matter-of-factly. "He can't do nothin' wit'chu, baby," he said in his strong Jersey Italian accent. "He's too light in da ass."

Mekhi nodded in agreement. Never in a million years did he think he was going to spend the remainder of his high school career at an all-boys school. St. Benedict's Preparatory School or "The Hive," as the boys called it, was an institution that had a phenomenal reputation for combining rigorous academic study with an emphasis on building a community whose members are responsible to one another for developing virtue, character, and talent. "What hurts my brother, hurts me" was the motto the boys lived by, and it was definitively the foundation in which Mekhi's friendship with his crew was built upon.

Curtis looked over at Mekhi for something more reassuring than a nod, but got nothing. It was a response very uncharacteristic of him. Normally, he would have something prolific to say to uplift his St. Benedict brother of his God-given gift. But at that moment, all he could think about was his mother. It had been three days since their fight. Since he'd seen or spoken to her. Three long days and not a phone call, text, or visit.

Jamie and Curtis were taken aback by Mekhi's silence. He hadn't told them what transpired between his mother and him. Jamie talked too much, and Curtis was too much of a narcissist to care. Carmine was the only one who Mekhi entrusted with that day's unfortunate events. He didn't judge him. He just listened. Like he always did.

"Yo, what up, Khi? You ain't got nuttin' philosophical to say, nigga?" Jamie teased, his Cheshire cat-like smile broad.

"Nah," Mekhi replied quietly.

"Why not?" Jamie asked, growing curious.

"Just don't." Mekhi shrugged. He wasn't in the mood for Jamie's prying. His friend could be as bad as a female when it came to asking questions. His persistence was unbelievable and annoying at the same time.

"But you always got somethin' to say," Jamie replied, his eyebrows knitted together.

"Well, today I don't," Mekhi responded sharply. "Is dat aiight wit'chu?

"No, it ain't aiight wit' me." Jamie snarled. "Our mans is havin' a muthafuckin' crisis, and you ain't got shit to say."

"Da world don't revolve around Curt, aiight?" Mekhi hollered. "Goddamn, man! I mean, shit! Why can't you just leave a nigga be, for once?"

"Ay, nigga—" Jamie began, his voice serious and deep.

"Nah, Jay! I don't wanna hear it," Mekhi howled. "Curt's problem ain't shit compared to mine! Real muthafuckin' talk, homie!"

Jamie and Curtis stood in astonishment. In all the years of them knowing Mekhi, they'd never seen him lose his cool. He was the most level-headed of the four—or so they thought.

"What kinda shit you goin' through? Huh?" Jamie

smirked. "What? You can't get ya backstroke right?"

"You're a clown, you know dat?" Mekhi growled.

"What?" Jamie stepped into Mekhi's personal space.

"You heard me, nigga," Mekhi jeered.

"Ay, yo, fuck you, you juvenile delinquent muthafucka." Jamie began to remove his backpack from his shoulders. "I'll fuck you up."

"See me, den, nigga." Mekhi crossed his arms at his chest. "I'm right here."

Jamie moved in closer, peering up at Mekhi.

"Ay, oh, oh!" Carmine and Curtis chimed in unison as they jumped in between the two. Curtis pulled Jamie away as he continued to hurl obscenities at Mekhi. He, in turn, mocked him with a smile.

"Dat nigga's a clown, C." Mekhi watched Curtis struggle to calm Jamie down.

"He ain't all bad. Can't let 'im get under ya skin like that, bro," Carmine professed. "You all right? "

"Yeah, I'm cool," Mekhi assured him.

"You sure?" Carmine asked earnestly.

"Yeah," Mekhi reassured him with an unyielding glance.

"All right." Carmine looked him over before turning his attention to the busy roadway.

Amongst the stream of cars flowing down Springfield Avenue was a pearl white Mercedes S Class. Carmine nudged his brother from another mother in the arm.

"Ay. That looks like ya mom's car," Carmine said.

"Where?" Mekhi asked, looking for the vehicle along the hectic main road.

"Right there." Carmine pointed. The woman behind the wheel was checking her eyes in the visor mirror.

Mekhi focused in on her. She shared his mother's face. It was indeed, her.

"Oh . . . yeah," he replied dryly.

"It's her, isn't it?" Carmine asked, staring at the car.

Mekhi nodded slowly. He continued to stare at his mother from across the street. He wanted her to look his way, to notice him. To pull out of line, pull over and beckon him to the car, so that he could get in and fall into her arms. He longed for her touch, for her love. The same love he fought against. As much grief as he gave her, she never missed a swim or track meet. *Never.* He didn't deserve her. And Mekhi knew it.

He was tired. Tired of fighting, . . .tired of being angry, . . . tired of the contempt he felt for her most of the time. His grandfather was the only father he'd ever had or known, and now that his health was failing, he had no one. He didn't know his biological father. His mother and the courts made sure of that. But he did know that the man tried to kill him. It wasn't a kept secret. He'd asked his mother at seven years old what the "thing" was on his back. The keloid. A little girl at the day camp he attended every summer pointed it out to him. So, she and his grandfather sat him down and explained that his father had done a very bad thing. He was sick and made a mistake by hurting him.

Of course, when Mekhi became of age, he went to his grandfather again and requested the entire, unfiltered story. Lorenzo advised that he was to never bring up the horrific events of that night in conversation with his mother. She was not to blame for his father's actions. Her only crime was loving a man who had a history of violence, something she truly knew nothing about. And for a long time, Mekhi didn't blame her, because that was his mother. And *his* mother was perfect.

His grandfather was not one to lie. Whatever he said was gospel, so he didn't question him. But now, he wished she'd fallen in love with someone else. Someone who wasn't crazy, so he'd have a man, a real man, to continue guiding him through this life.

Mekhi's gaze suddenly met with Karma's as she turned toward the group of boys. He saw her lips quivering and noticed she had her half-tinted Chanel sunglasses on. She only wore those when she was trying to hide. Had she been crying?

The light turned green. The cars ahead of her began to move, and the person behind her honked his horn, snapping her out of her trance. She pulled off slowly, and then accelerated midway down the long, congested road.

"Looks like she's on her way to *Afro-Cubana*," Carmine guessed.

"Probably," Mekhi replied, biting the inside of his cheek.

Carmine turned toward his troubled friend and threw his muscled arm around his neck. "It's gonna be okay."

Mekhi gave him a wary glance.

"It is. You'll see." Carmine smiled.

Curtis and Jamie made their way back. Still angry, Jamie refused to look at Mekhi. Luckily, something worth his fancy caught his attention.

"Yo, who's dat wit' Desi?" Jamie asked, while throwing and then catching his baseball.

The boys followed his eyes.

The unknown young lady walking with the redhead was just as tall as she was, but much thicker in the hip and thigh area. Her wavy, black hair was pulled back into a tight bun as well. Her chocolate skin glistened against the raindrops that fell upon her face. Her full lips spread into a wide smile, revealing teeth the color of ivory . She had a small gap in between her top front teeth just like Desi. Her beauty was captivating. It was au natural and that's what captured Mekhi's attention the most. He could tell she was a good girl like his cousin. All of her friends were. Well, before he and his friends got a hold of them, ruining them forever.

The girls approached them with broad smiles and giggles.

"Hey, y'all," Desi waved, looking up at each of them.

"Hey, Des," they replied in unison, with the exception of Mekhi.

"Hey, big head," she teased, looping her arm with his.

"'Sup?" Mekhi said with a cool nod.

"The sky," she joked.

"Aww, dat was cheeks," Carmine, Curtis, and Jamie exclaimed, dismissing her with the wave of their hands.

"Oh, whatever." She grinned .

"Straight ass," Curtis stated.

"Shut up, Curt." Desi smirked.

"Make me."

"No, that's okay. You might like it." she said, seriously.

"Nah, I *know* I will," Curt replied, even more serious as his eyes remained on Desi.

She searched his pretty, black sateen face for the humor she thought was behind his response. Yet she found nothing but a lustful gaze. His eyes were calling for hers to connect and accept all that he wanted to offer.

Mekhi looked over at his comrade in utter disbelief. "Word, fam'?" Mekhi challenged with stern eyes.

"I'm jus' playin', nigga."

"Yeah, aiight." Mekhi sucked his teeth, knowing better.

"Okayyy," Desi interrupted nervously.

Mekhi made a mental note to keep a close eye on Curtis, before slowly looking away and acknowledging his cousin once again.

"Who's ya friend?" Jamie asked, licking his lips.

Desiree and her girlfriend raised their brows in response to Jamie's lewd action.

"This is my girl, Ekua," Desi replied proudly.

"Hi," Ekua said with a soft southern drawl.

"'Sup," the boys responded.

"Nice name," Jamie said, giving her a once-over.

"Thank you," she responded, shifting her weight to one leg. Suddenly uncomfortable, Ekua took her coat out of her bookbag and put it on.

"What's that . . . like Haitian or somethin'?" Jamie asked.

The girls smirked in response, embarrassed for him. His ignorance was killing any chances he thought he had with her.

"You mean, is it French? Haitian is a nationality, genius," Desi exclaimed haughtily.

"I mean, yeah. You know what the fuck I mean, Des,'" Jamie replied acutely .

"It's African," Mekhi responded.

Ekua looked over at Mekhi, tilting her head slightly to the side. "He speaks." She grinned.

Desiree and the boys watched the unexpected exchange between the two.

"It means born on a Wednesday. Right?" Mekhi asked.

"Right. But I was actually born on a Friday."

Mekhi remained solemn, but nodded in response to her cute wit.

"Are you all right?" she asked, locking eyes with him.

Mekhi wished she stopped looking at him with those mesmerizing bedroom eyes .

"Why do you ask?" he countered, genuinely confused.

"Your grandfather," Ekua replied, keeping her eyes

fixed on him.

"Oh. Yeah. I'm straight," Mekhi replied.

"Okay. Well, I hope he pulls through."

"Thanks," Mekhi mumbled.

"Well, we're out," Desi proclaimed, breaking the discomfort within the group. "See you later," she said to her cousin, extending her arms. He bent down so she could wrap them around his neck. The two embraced in a hug. She kissed him on the cheek thereafter.

"Aww," the boys teased.

"Yo, shut up," Mekhi and Desi spat.

"Ay, where y'all goin'?" Jamie asked with an attitude.

"Away from you!" Desi threw over her shoulder, walking away from the quartet.

"Damn." Carmine chuckled.

"Man, shut up," Jamie snickered in embarrassment.

"Wait!" Curtis yelled after them.

The girls turned back in their direction. "What?" Desi asked with sass.

"Y'all comin' to the game?" Curt asked with hopeful eyes.

"Maybe!" Desi yelled back. "Maybe not!" she teased, turning away.

A small grin grew along Curtis' face.

Mekhi shook his head as he watched his cousin and her friend saunter away. He made a mental note to speak to Desi about his disapproval of the flirting between her and

Curtis. Then he focused on Ekua again. If his life wasn't in such shambles, he would have made an advance before Jamie did.

Taking a moment, Mekhi thought about all that transpired. Ekua hadn't taken to Jamie too well. Maybe there was hope for him after all. Maybe there wasn't. He didn't know. Whatever. Females were the farthest things from his mind. He needed to know how his grandfather and mother were.

What am I going to do if Papa dies? He thought. *And how da fuck am I gonna make shit right wit' my moms?*

Chapter 5

Heartbroken, Karma sat at her father's bedside with his ripened hand in hers. She ran her thumbs along his thick, protruding veins as she closed her eyes, awaiting the arrival of the funeral directors. His transition hadn't been a kind one. She let her mind wander back to the day she and Mekhi's lives changed forever. That day at the house where he lay on the floor, helpless and alone. To the moment he let go under her touch. It seemed as if the paramedics would never come. Ten minutes had felt like an eternity. When they did arrive, they were accompanied by the fire and police departments, while she was being held hostage by hysteria and perplexity. There was too much noise, too many people, too much commotion for one person.

That was five days ago. Today was Thursday, October 28th . Her father made his transition at 5:53 p.m. He was seventy-two years old. Karma had lived at the hospital for five long days and four sleepless nights. She lifted her eyes from his hand and settled them on his peaceful face. Seventy-two was too young to die. Fifty-four was too young to die. Both of her parents, two good people who made bad decisions, and succumbed to the consequences of their actions. Her father never got over the passing of her mother. Neither of them had. But she, unlike him, handled it better. He sought refuge in the arms of hard, unapologetic liquor. She thought he'd stopped years ago, but she'd recently found bottles of whiskey and vodka in Mekhi's closet, of all places. Sixteen years of drinking led to five days of rapid deterioration. Four of those five days were spent with him slipping in and out of consciousness. On one of those nights, he recognized his only daughter with two eyes, one tear, one smile and two words: "Hi, honey." One day of uninterrupted moaning in untreatable, uncontrollable pain. One second of abrupt silence that turned into two seconds, then three, the fourth evolving into a minute which transformed into many.

Karma closed her eyes and shuddered in response to the silence that crept into the place of the incessant moaning she'd become accustomed to. She dropped her head and began to weep as she accepted the transition of her beloved father. She was alone now. No mother, no father. Karma never told anyone that she often wondered how she was going to handle his passing. She'd thought his death wasn't going to be as traumatic and horrendous as her mother's. Oh, how sadly mistaken she was. He'd suffered a great deal, and he'd initially died in her arms.

How am I going to move on from this? She wasn't. She would, instead, carry it with her until it was her turn to pass on. Her son, and other surviving loved ones would make attempts to cover her emotional wounds with words of comfort, hugs, and kisses, prayers and photographs. But when night fell and all was still and she was left alone with her thoughts, Karma would curl into a ball and cry into a pillow. She would hold herself, wishing her arms were that of her father's and mother's.

"Playing a nationally-renowned schedule, including seven teams ranking in the Top 25 in the country, St. Benedict's is on their way to the ESPN Rise National High School Invitational," mentioned one of the two ESPN commentators sitting on the sideline.

The Prudential Center's 18,711-seated basketball arena was filled to capacity. People had come from all over the state to see the face-off between Roselle Catholic and St. Benedict Prep Academy. The Newark National Invitational was one of New Jersey's premier high school sporting events, and Curtis had led his team there with the expectation to win. The season had been full of surprising upsets thus far. Curtis knew where they'd been going wrong. There was no trust amongst them. After losing last week's game to Blair Academy, the team sat down and talked about the importance of trust. The offense, defense, and what the coaches were doing was going to play a big part in the outcome tonight. Curtis was going to put an end to any doubts the naysayers had about him or his teammates.

Mekhi, exhausted from swimming practice that afternoon, stood beside Carmine and Jamie in the midst of a sea of Gray Bees, both young and old. The trio proudly watched their brother fly swiftly up and down the court with ease. The team had finally gotten it together after a rough first quarter, putting forth one of the best offensive and defensive performances of the season. They were utilizing their bench and scoring with tremendous balance. Seven of the players scored at least six points. Curtis showcased an array of scoring skills via spot-up three-pointers, transition dunks and tough two-point shots. He was pacing the Gray Bees throughout the game, scoring multiple buckets in each quarter and proving to be a vital piece at the core of their defense. He was on his way to finishing with thirty points.

"Look! Look! Dat nigga's not even breakin' a sweat!" Jamie yelled excitedly.

"I told 'im not to worry about that Holmes chump!" Carmine countered.

Mekhi unscrewed the top to his Gatorade bottle and took a sip of the refreshing beverage. He licked his lips as he placed the top back on. As happy as he was to be there supporting his friend, he couldn't stay focused long enough to really appreciate the moment. All Mekhi could think about was his grandfather. He hadn't seen him since the day he collapsed. Visiting him at the hospital wasn't an option. He couldn't stand the smell. The mixture of cleaning products and sickness. He'd visited Desi once, years ago after she had hernia surgery and that infamous smell stayed with him long after her release.

He couldn't bring himself to see the man who'd raised him as his own, lying in a bed, motionless and unresponsive. So he stayed away. His aunt had kept him abreast of his grandfather's condition as it gradually changed from bad to worse over the course of five days. She'd speak to his mother, then relay the messages to him.

The end was near. She'd told him so. But he didn't believe there was any special way a person could truly prepare for the loss of a loved one. Especially, not someone as close to him as his grandfather.

Mekhi could feel his eyes brimming with tears as he continued to think about his hero. He closed them, placing his thumb and index finger in each corner. The shot clock buzzer rang, forcing him out of his reverie. The third quarter was over. As Mekhi blinked back his sadness, he looked up at one of the exits and decided he needed to take a walk.

"Ay." He nudged Carmine in the arm. "I'm gonna go take a walk. Get a pretzel or somethin'."

Carmine looked over at his best friend and noticed his eyes were glossed over.

"You want me to go wit' you?"

"Nah, I'm good," Mekhi lied.

"You sure?" Carmine asked, knowing better.

"Yeah." Mekhi nodded. "Want me to get you somethin'?"

Carmine eyed him a moment before responding. "Nah, I got my heart set on the food at the diner. We're still goin', right?"

"Absolutely," Mekhi reassured him.

"All right. Don't get lost, man," Carmine teased.

"Never dat." Mekhi smiled.

The two performed their secret handshake before Mekhi excused himself and began to move through the crowd.

"Where you goin', nigga?" Jamie yelled to Mekhi's back.

"To da bathroom!" Mekhi threw over his shoulder.

Jamie sucked his teeth as he watched Mekhi disappear.

The long corridor was just as crowded as the arena. Mekhi stuck out like a sore thumb. His blue eyes capturing the attention of a number of girls. A mouthy Latina standing with her friends by a decorated vendor's table pursed her lips in delight as Mekhi walked by.

"Damn. I'd like to climb that," she purred, sucking on a cherry blow pop.

Mekhi turned around and gave her a dimpled grin. She had a lot of nerve to say such a thing so loudly. He liked it. She was the type of girl he fancied the most, because she would be forced to back up her words.

"You got his attention, girl," her heavyset girlfriend exclaimed.

Mekhi strolled back in the trio's direction, stopping in front of the girl who made the comment. She was dressed in a black, long-sleeved mesh top and skinny jeans. Her red bra matched the pair of classic Air Jordans on her small feet. Her face was heavily caked with make-up and her long ponytail was sinfully oiled.

"What's good, mami?" Mekhi queried, piercing his blue eyes down on her.

"Nothin' much," she replied, raising a seductive brow. "Those your real eyes?"

"Yup." He nodded.

"They're pretty." She grinned.

"Not as pretty as you." Mekhi countered. She blushed.

"Mm-hmm. I bet you say that to every bitch that comes your way." She smirked.

"Only if it applies." He grinned. Mekhi had much game. She had to applaud him for it. "So, tell me again about you wantin' to ride dis," he urged, crossing his arms.

"Really, Khi?" a familiar voice asked from behind him.

Mekhi turned, looking down into the faces of a disgusted Desiree and stunned Ekua.

"This is how you get down?" Desi asked, her brows knitting together. "Fuckin' wit' street urchins like them?"

"Who the fuck you callin' street urchin, hoe?" the vulgar-mouthed girl derided, pushing past Mekhi.

"You bitch!" Desi spat back.

The Latina's friends charged at Desi, but Mekhi blocked them with his massive frame.

"Ay yo, chill. Chill!" he urged, with his arms spread a mile wide.

"Fuckin' scallywag," Desi hissed, mushing the girl in the head. She staggered backward.

"Bitch!" the group of rowdy girls hollered.

Desi, unmoved by their anger, laughed incredulously as a number of security personnel appeared and dragged them away.

"This isn't over, bitch!" the incensed girl muttered.

"Whateva!" Desi yelled back, not the least worried.

Mekhi turned toward Desi and looked at her in disbelief. "Ay, yo, what da fuck is wrong wit'chu, Des?"

"Me? What the fuck is wrong wit' you?" she fired back.

"Ain't shit wrong wit' me!" Mekhi furrowed his brows.

"Obviously, there is if you hollerin' at that trick!"

"You don't even know da girl."

"I ain't gotta know her to know that she's a hoe and probably got somethin'," she stated, matter-of-factly.

"She's right," Ekua chimed quietly.

Mekhi, embarrassed that Ekua had witnessed the explicit conversation, struggled to regain his composure. "I wasn't lookin' to get any ass from her," he admitted. "I just wanted to see how far she was gonna go wit' her teasin'."

"Okay," Ekua replied, dispassionately.

"Okay?" Mekhi asked in confusion.

"Yeah. Okay. If that's the truth, then I'm not going to question you." Ekua shrugged. "I don't know you well enough to know if you're lying or not."

"Well, I'm not," he insisted gently. "I wouldn't lie to you. Not about somethin' like that."

Mekhi's face softened, and his body relaxed under Ekua's gaze. She had a hold on him like no other. It was as if he didn't want her to perceive him as something that he wasn't—a player. Or to think little of him because of how he responded to the attention he received from other girls, experienced and inexperienced. Ekua's opinion of him *mattered*. And his cousin Desi thought that was wonderful.

Ekua blushed as she shifted her weight from one leg to the other. She wished he'd stopped looking at her with those eyes. They were so intense. Looking through her more so than at her. For the first time in her teenaged life, she felt insecure. And the boy she'd begun to dream about at night was the cause of it.

"So, where y'all sittin'?" Mekhi asked, breaking the silence between them.

"In section three," Ekua uttered.

"Oh, aiight." Mekhi smiled.

Suddenly, he felt a vibration in one of his coat pockets.

"Excuse me," he said as he took his cell phone out and looked at the name scrolled across the screen. Any sense of calm Mekhi may have had up until that moment immediately went away. Desi and Ekua noticed the grim expression on his face.

"What's the matter?" Desi asked, in a subtle panic.

Mekhi held his finger up as he answered the call. "Hello?" he breathed solemnly into the receiver.

"Mekhi, baby?" Indigo sniffled on the other end. "He's gone."

Chapter 6

Karma walked out of The Family Funeral Home arm-in-arm with Indigo. The women patted their wet faces with tissue. Seeing her father in that casket was such a hurtful thing. Nonetheless, an inspection had to be done. Karma didn't want to be unpleasantly surprised on the day of his homegoing. Thankfully, she wouldn't, because they'd done a beautiful job with him. He was dressed in a sharp black Calvin Klein suit with a pink paisley print tie and matching handkerchief set in his jacket pocket. He held his favorite photograph of her mother in his hands. Karma requested that the photo be placed in the casket with him. She didn't know the funeral director was going to take her request a step further and lay it with him. Karma fell apart. Indigo wrapped her arm tightly around her cousin's waist and cried along with her. She'd lost her own father two years ago, so she was familiar with Karma's pain. The inevitable separation between parent and child, father and daughter.

She stroked her father's clean-shaven head for a while, before leaning down and pressing her forehead against his. She held his head with her left hand, while cupping his right cheek in the other. He was cold, but she could still feel the softness of his skin under her touch. Karma closed her eyes and gently kissed the treasured soldier on his forehead. He was finally at peace, eternally with his wife.

Karma decided upon an all-in-one day service, consisting of a two-hour viewing that transitioned into a closed casket funeral. She believed the one-day celebration would be easier to handle for both herself and Mekhi. *Mekhi.* Karma hadn't spoken to her son since Saturday night. She'd packed his bags and left them at the door.

"How's Mekhi?" Karma asked, breaking the silence between them.

"Quiet," Indigo admitted, wiping her nose. "He doesn't say much to Stuff or me. Speaks mostly to Desi."

"Oh," Karma replied, sadly.

"Why don't you come by and have dinner with us tonight?" Indigo suggested warmly. "Talk to your baby."

Karma gave the invitation some thought. "I can't face him," she confessed.

Indigo squeezed her cousin's arm supportively. "And vice versa," she proclaimed. "But you're the mother. And it's your job to lead by example, right?"

Karma nodded.

"Well, then come on over and show him how it's done," she insisted.

As Karma looked out onto Clinton Avenue, traffic flowed heavily in both directions. She internalized her cousin's spoken truth. Indigo was right, but she wasn't ready to face Mekhi. She didn't know what to say to him, nor did she trust herself in his presence. *What if I go off again?*

"He needs his suit for tomorrow," she remembered aloud.

"So, bring it with you when you come," Indigo replied.

"I haven't decided if I'm coming or not," Karma countered. "I have plans already and—"

"Oh, now you have plans? What plans could you possibly have tonight?" Indigo asked, irritated.

"That's none of your business," Karma spat.

"The hell it isn't. This whole jacked-up situation is my business. And you want to know why? Because you made it my business."

"I'm not doing this with you." Karma unlocked her arm from Indigo's.

"Oh, yes you are." Indigo grabbed Karma's arm forcefully.

Karma looked down at her cousin's hand, then back into her face as if she'd lost her mind.

"Let go of my arm," she demanded, tugging it.

"No," Indigo coolly replied.

"Let go!"

"'No! I asked you a question!"

A stare-off ensued. Karma was mentally and emotionally drained. *Why can't Indigo accept that I'm just not ready to see the damage I inflicted on Mekhi?* Not so much the physical this time, she'd seen that the night she threw him out of the house. It was the mental and emotional scars she would be able to see in his eyes that she couldn't deal with. She was still being haunted by her reckless behavior from two years past. Their relationship was strained to this very day because of it.

Karma just wasn't ready for "the look." Mekhi no longer held her in high regard because of what she'd done. And it hurt her to the core of her being.

"Well?" Indigo asked, her eyebrows raised.

"I'm having company," Karma said tersely, snatching her arm out of Indigo's grasp.

"Who?" Indigo pried.

"Who do you think?"

Indigo took a step back and crossed her arms at her chest. "Hassan?"

Karma smirked and raised her eyebrows.

"I can't believe you," Indigo said with squinted eyes.

"What? I'm not allowed to have company now?"

"No, not at a time like this. Getting your back blown out tonight as a means of forgetting about what the hell is going on between you and your son is not the damn answer!"

Amazed, Karma smiled, her pearl white teeth sparkling against the cold rain. "Wow. I never thought you, of all people, would think so little of me." She retrieved her car keys out of her pocketbook, then pressed the unlock button on her alarm. Karma opened the door, and then settled behind the wheel. She slammed the door thereafter, placed her key in the ignition, and headed out of the parking lot.

Indigo cut Karma deeply with her words. She stood, running her hand along her neat French-braid and fingering a number of loose white hairs back into place as she watched the cousin she considered more as a sister race down the street. Hurting her feelings hadn't been her intention. But she meant what she said. Karma needed to focus on the situation at hand. And whether she wanted to admit it to herself or not, Hassan was a distraction. As far as Indigo was concerned, he wasn't a good one.

She gathered her thoughts as she stepped into her jeep and made her way home. It was her turn to cook tonight, and she was already an hour behind in preparation.

Stuff excused himself from the dining table before following Indigo into the kitchen. He walked up behind her, pressing himself against her and whispering something explicit in her ear. His sweet nothings caused her to giggle like a giddy schoolgirl. She turned and placed her arms around his neck. Then embraced him with a passionate kiss. Stuff set his hands on her firm backside and squeezed it, causing soft moans to escape from her mouth. She'd cooked a meal fit for kings, and he wanted her to know how grateful he was to have her as his wife and the mother of his daughter. They'd been together for twenty years, and Indigo looked as good as she did then, now. Slight weight gain and all. Stuff did as well. Even with his potbelly, crow's feet and salt and pepper goatee, Indigo nevertheless thought he was the sexiest man alive. The two were still very much madly in love; creating not only a beautiful child, but successful careers.

Indigo owned and ran one of the most successful dance academies in the state, and Stuff sat as the founder and president of one of the country's leading independently black-owned financial institutions. The Davis' had done well for themselves.

Mekhi, along with Desi and Maggie , watched the freak fest from the dining room. Mekhi, taken aback by the couple's unadulterated public display of affection, cleared his throat in discomfort. He looked back and forth from his cousin to his great-aunt and noticed they were unfazed by the kiss. And for the first time in a long time, he thought about his father. He wondered if he ever kissed his mother like that. If the man loved her so much that he'd dare someone to challenge the way he showed his appreciation. Mekhi guessed he would never know.

"Yo," he said, shifting in his seat.

"It'll be over soon." Desi laughed. "Believe me. That's nothing compared to what you might hear later on tonight."

"What?" Mekhi squirmed.

"Nothing." Desi giggled.

"Me so glad you're here for a while, Mekhi," a gray dreadlocked Maggie said and smiled.

"Yeah. I jus' wish it was unda betta circumstances, Auntie." Mekhi sulked.

"Me known your mother all she life. And me know her sorry for what she done to you de other night."

"Well, she ain't actin' like she sorry. She ain't called or

came over here to apologize," he countered with attitude.

"Her will in she own time."

"No disrespect, Auntie. But I don't give a fuck no more."

"Ay!" Stuff shouted from the kitchen, before storming into the dining room.

"Fuck her!" Mekhi growled.

"What in the—" Indigo said, following her husband into the dining room.

"Da fuck you jus' say, man?" Stuff snarled, snatching him out of his chair and throwing him against a nearby wall.

"Oh my God!" Indigo and Maggie screamed in unison.

"Daddy, no!" Desi yelled.

Mekhi held on to his uncle's fists tightly. Stuff had him pinned up, his feet dangling beneath him.

"Don't you eva curse ya muthafuckin' muva again, you undastand me?" Stuff thundered. "You undastand me, nigga?" He shook him violently. "You wouldn't even fuckin' be here if it wasn't for her! You know dat? She saved ya muthafuckin' life!"

Indigo rushed over to them and placed her hands on Stuff's. "Baby, let him go. He didn't mean it."

"Da hell he didn't," he sneered, never taking his eyes off of the shaken boy.

"Stuff, baby, please." Indigo begged to no avail.

"Not until he apologizes," Stuff seethed.

Mekhi choked back a set a tears that were threatening to fall. His body trembled under his uncle's grasp.

"All I'm sayin', Unc, is . . . is if she loved me like y'all say she does, she'd be here right now," he sputtered nervously.

Stuff regained his composure and released him, setting him back down onto the floor. He felt sorry for the overgrown boy. He had no control over his emotions.

He was simply a lost soul.

"She does love you, Khi. But you fucked up. *Bad.* And you can't expect her to just get over what you did, overnight. Forgiveness takes time, my nigga. You gotta earn dat shit," Stuff schooled him. "Now apologize for disrespectin' ya muva and mine at my muthafuckin' table."

"I apologize," Mekhi mumbled.

Karma lay beneath Hassan's massive six-foot-four, 380-pound frame, releasing moans of passion and tears of loss. Her lover and companion had been away in Los Angeles on business. A former running back for Penn State and the Philadelphia Eagles, he flew back and forth from Jersey to L.A. every two weeks to perform his job as a commentator on SportsCenter. The two spent the majority of their relationship apart. The cell phone being their lifeline.

Hassan held her hands above her head with his left, while holding her left leg in the crux of his right arm. Karma bit down on her bottom lip as he glided in and out of her. He had great control of his massive body. He handled her much like a football. Karma barely felt the ultra-thin condom on his penis. She hoped he hadn't been slick and taken it off between position changes. He was good for that.

He opened his eyes and took in her beauty, then leaned down and pressed his lips against hers. She invaded his mouth with her tongue. "I missed you," he whispered in her ear, driving her crazy with his long, deep strokes.

"I . . . unh . . ." she panted. "Mmm."

Releasing her hands, Hassan allowed her to wrap her sweat-drenched arms around his thick neck. He moved his hands behind her upper back and waist, cradling her. Karma wrapped her legs around his torso, locking her ankles. She knew the end was near, and she was going to hold on tight for the ride. Hassan buried his face in her neck and began to pound into her. Her cries of passion were driving him wild.

"It's yours, baby," he moaned. "Mmm, enjoy it."

Karma submitted to his will. She threw her head back and screamed his name in sheer pleasure as a wave of ecstasy coursed through her body and poured out onto him. Her tongue found his ear lobe. She sucked it, then held it between her teeth.

"Aww, shit!" Hassan murmured into her ear.

Just as quickly as he spoke, an electric pulse of euphoria shot through him and into the condom. He let out a loud, blissful cry as he pumped into her until there was nothing left to deposit.

Karma placed her hands on his wet, chestnut-brown face and settled her eyes on his. He had such beautiful eyelashes. They were so long and thick. Hassan returned her warm gaze. He was equally enamored with her eyes. He'd had his share of beautiful women, but none of them compared to Karma. She was in a class all by herself.

"I love you," she said, tears brimming in her eyes.

"I love you more," he replied, brushing her flushed cheeks with his thumbs.

The two embraced in a slow, tender kiss. Tears fell from Karma's eyes onto Hassan's fingers. "Don't cry, baby," he pleaded, wiping them away.

Unlike Karma, Hassan refused to admit that their relationship was wrong, their love forbidden. Their liaison had been wrong from the very beginning. And as much as Karma tried to keep her distance, Hassan always found a way to close the space between them.

"Want me to leave?" he asked.

Karma shook her head. "No," she wept. "Promise me you never will."

"I promise," Hassan stated seriously. He scooped her into his arms, before rolling onto his back. She settled into the comfort of his strong embrace. He held her close, and he held her tight, allowing her to be dependent on him, to be helpless, to completely fall apart for the first time in their relationship. *How could something so wrong feel so right?*

Chapter 7

Funerals . . . he hated funerals. Mekhi stared out of the window in the backseat of Stuff's jeep as Desi held his hand. The day had finally come to put his grandfather to rest. He barely slept the previous night. He had such a hard time at his paternal grandmother's funeral years ago. Mekhi believed she died more so from a broken heart, than the cancer the doctors diagnosed her with. She'd spent many a night mourning the loss of his father. Even though he was alive and well, he wasn't free. She blamed herself for his ill-mind, for his incarceration. Mekhi really felt badly for her. So when she passed, he embraced it. For she was finally free.

Stuff turned onto Elmwynd Drive and drove into the long driveway that sat beside the modest Tudor. He put the car in park, and then shut it off.

"All right." Indigo sighed. She was dressed in a beautiful black cowl neck dress and matching duster. Her black and white hair was pulled back into a ponytail. She unbuckled her belt and took her purse into her hands. Stuff, Desi, and Mekhi followed suit. The family exited the vehicle, closing the doors behind them. Stuff and Desi were dressed in black as well. He wore a Hugo Boss suit with a wool trench coat. Desi donned a cute sweater dress with tights and a long peacoat from Boden.

Indigo stepped up to the door and placed her key into the top lock, then the bottom. She placed her hand on the doorknob and turned it. She gently pushed the door open and entered. Stuff, Desi, and Mekhi followed. Mekhi closed the door behind them.

"*Prima?*" she yelled from the foyer.

"Upstairs!" Karma replied from her master bathroom. "Make yourselves comfortable!"

"Okay!" Indigo responded. She turned toward Mekhi and placed her hand on his cheek. "Go upstairs and get ready, okay?" Indigo smiled sadly.

Mekhi nodded.

"It's going to be all right," she assured him, stroking his face.

Mekhi nodded again. He looked up in the direction of the stairwell, bracing himself for the unknown. His feet began to move beneath him, leading him up the stairs.

"I'm fuckin' starvin'," Stuff admitted, unexpectedly.

Indigo cut her eyes at her husband as their daughter covered a smile with her hand. "I asked you if you wanted me to cook you a third sausage, egg and cheese sandwich with grits. You said no," she replied in disbelief.

"I lied," he confessed.

Indigo walked away, sucking her teeth.

Karma sat on the edge of her bed with her eyes closed, silently praying. She could hear Indigo and Stuff bickering downstairs and the water from Mekhi's shower running. Hassan left earlier that morning, leaving her alone with her thoughts. She'd done exactly what Indigo said she would. She'd succumbed to Hassan's shameless call. He'd teased and pleased, slapped and pulled, squeezed and sucked everything out of her. And she enjoyed it . . . every single moment of it.

Her body ached. Karma prayed for strength to get through the day. She prayed that the tension between her and Mekhi would be lifted. She prayed that the transition from having a patriarch in their lives to not having one at all would be smooth.

Mekhi's shower cut off. Karma slowly opened her eyes and exhaled. She looked down at her watch. The limo would be there soon. She rose from the bed and smoothed her form-fitting black, sleeveless dress down. Karma walked over to her body-length floor mirror and adjusted her mother's pearl necklace around her neck. She ran her hands over her slicked back hair and checked her flawless make-up a final time. Turning, she retrieved her suit jacket and pocketbook from the bed. She walked out into the hall and looked across the way at Mekhi's bedroom door. Karma placed her things on the miniature pillar at the top of the banister and proceeded to her son's bedroom. She knocked gently on the door.

"Come in," Mekhi instructed, his tone low and sad. Karma turned the knob, gradually opening the door. Mekhi stood with his back to her. He was tucking his shirt into his pants. Karma took a step forward, then another, then another. Mekhi zipped and buttoned his well-tailored slacks. He slid his size fifteen feet into his loafers, and then flung his tie around his neck. Karma walked up behind him, placing her hands on his shoulders. Mekhi briefly looked over his left shoulder, before slowly turning to face his mother. He avoided all eye contact with her, keeping his head bowed.

Searching for her son's eyes, she gently took his face into her hands and raised it. Mekhi refused to open his eyes. He clenched and unclenched his jaw in an attempt to keep himself from crumbling under her touch. Karma began rubbing his cheeks with her thumbs. She studied his healed skin, the arch in his brows, the length of his lashes, the fullness of his lips, the waves in his hair. *I have birthed the most beautifully flawed creature*, she thought.

"I'm sorry," she whispered.

Gone.

Mekhi lost all control and wept. Karma brought him into her and laid his head on her shoulder. Mekhi wrapped his arms around his mother, holding on to her, never wanting to let her go. She broke free from her composure and cried with her baby boy. Mekhi's legs gave way, causing them to fall to their knees. Mother . . . son . . . *reunited.*

With his back against the wall, Mekhi sat at a table in a

corner of his mother's Montclair-based restaurant. He loved this location so much better than the home-based one. Its architectural design was inspired by 16th Century Havana and the Cuban Baroque era. The entrance was lined with palm fronds and coconuts that led into three dimly lit dining rooms and an outdoor courtyard. His mother incorporated traditional Spanish-Moorish features such as patios, fountains, and decorative tiles in the floors and walls. It was fitted with grand colonnaded *portales* (porches) to provide shade and shelter from the diverse weather conditions, and *rejas*, metal bars, were secured over open window panes to allow for a freer circulation of air. Other distinctive Cuban features included *vitrales*—multi-colored glass panes fitted above the entryways to pleasantly diffuse the summer season's sunrays. And unlike *Afro-Cubana, Soleil's* had all male servers who wore bright blue *guayabera* shirts and Panama hats.

He watched his friends indulge in their choice of Cuban or soul food dishes. He wasn't hungry. Far from it. He couldn't understand how people could eat after hours of mourning. How they set aside their grief to eat. So he just picked at the plate his mother made for him. He watched her work the room, bouncing from one guest to another, thanking them for coming. Then managing the staff with great poise and ease. Mekhi didn't know half of the people in the room. He knew his family, of course. The Mayor of Orange and the family's priest, Father Pacella. He knew the manager of the crisis center, his mother's Olympic relay team members, and his grandfather's closest friends, all retired military dressed in their uniforms. But outside of them, he had no clue who the other fifty people were.

Mekhi unloosened his tie, then took a sip out of his glass of non-alcoholic sangria. It had been a long, emotional day. The service was beautiful, and his mother had held up well. But he hadn't. He crumbled the moment he laid eyes on his grandfather in that casket. And he had yet to recover.

"Thanks for comin' today, y'all," Mekhi said just above a whisper.

"What hurts my brother hurts me," they expressed wholeheartedly in unison.

"Word up." Jamie nodded.

"We're family, baby. Any time," Carmine said.

"That's right," Curtis concluded.

Mekhi nodded with a small smile.

"It was a beautiful service, man. Beautiful," Carmine continued.

"Yeah. I liked the part when they presented your mom with the flag. That was official," Curtis chimed in with a mouthful of food.

"And da nigga playin' dat song at da cemetery," Jamie added.

"You mean *Taps*." Carmine laughed.

"Yeah. Dat shit was sad as fuck but tight all at da same time." Jamie chuckled.

Mekhi thought the same thing as he watched the young soldier with the bugle horn stand in the distance, blowing honor into that instrument. Calling on all who served this country with great courage.

"I'm goin' into da service after we graduate," Mekhi uttered as he continued to pick at his food.

"What?" they all asked at the same time.

"Wait a minute," Carmine began. "When did you make this decision?"

"Been thinkin' about it for a while. My grandfather and I talked about it a lot. When he was here," Mekhi admitted.

"Well, I think it's an honorable thing to do," Curtis admitted. "I support you, Khi."

"Thanks, Curt. Means a lot." Mekhi nodded coolly.

"Well, I don't," Carmine confessed. "You know how your mom feels about the military."

"She'll get over it." Mekhi shrugged. "She'll have to."

"Dat's some dumb shit," Jamie professed.

"What?" Mekhi asked with much attitude.

"You heard me, nigga," Jamie said. "You got da top universities afta you right now, sponsorship from da biggest fashion companies in da fuckin' world, and da chance to be on da Olympic swim team next year. You gonna give all dat shit up to be a G.I. muthafuckin' Joe?"

"You callin' my grandfather a toy soldier, nigga?" Mekhi asked, with the tilt of his head.

"Nah, nigga. I'm callin' *you* a toy soldier," Jamie corrected. "In fact, you're the wooden one from the muthafuckin' Nutcracka."

Without warning, Mekhi jumped up from his chair,

took Jamie by his shirt collar, and dragged him across the table onto the floor. He unmercifully pummeled him. Blood splattered, staining his face and shirt. Carmine and Curtis struggled to pull Mekhi off the bloodied boy.

Karma, who was in the midst of conversing with one of her serving staff members, snapped her head in the direction of the commotion. She saw Stuff, her uncle, and a couple of other men jump in between the four boys. Tables turned, chairs were thrown, and glass broke as everyone toppled over one another.

"Ahhh, *coño!*" Miguel yelled, grabbing his wrist. The palm of his cooking hand was severed.

Karma ran over and escorted him to another area in the room, sitting him down thereafter. *"Manténgalo en esa posición,"* she urged as she snatched a cloth napkin off the table and tied it around his hand. "Someone call 911, please?" Karma requested in a panic.

Seeing her uncle's severed hand took her back to the night she attacked her other uncle with the neck of a champagne bottle after discovering he'd been abusing her aunt. Miguel had gotten caught in the middle of that fight as well. Several nerves had been damaged, and he had to undergo surgery. It took several months of physical therapy for him to regain full usage of his hand. Karma never forgave herself for cutting him. It had been an accident, but she still beat herself up over it every time she saw him struggle to pick up something.

"I will!" a female voice responded.

"My arm!" she heard another voice call out.

The crowd began to disperse. Jamie lay on the floor in the fetal position, writhing in pain and holding his arm. The one he pitched with.

"I hope I broke dat shit!" Mekhi growled as Stuff dragged him away to the courtyard.

"Shut up! Shut up!" Stuff snarled in his ear.

The remaining mourners aided Jamie as Carmine and Curtis straightened their disheveled clothes and assisted the maintenance workers with cleaning up the broken dining furniture and drinkware.

"What da fuck is wrong wit' chu, Khi!" Stuff asked as he watched Mekhi punch the air.

"Dat bitch ass nigga called me a wooden soldier, Unc'!" Mekhi confessed.

"So that gave you the right to tear up my goddamn dining room? Because he called you a name?" Karma asked, storming into the piazza. "To disrespect your grandfather's memory and fight *today* of all days?"

Mekhi paced back and forth, eyeing the woman who gave him life. This wasn't the right time or place to tell her what he and his grandfather decided years ago.

"*Tio's* hand is sliced open because of your shit!" Karma continued.

"I'm goin' into da army after I graduate, aiight?" Mekhi huffed .

"What!" Karma asked, her brows knitting together.

"I told da fellaz what I'm gonna to do, and dat pussy ass nigga disrespected me. He disrespected me, and he disrespected Papa's legacy by callin' me a muthafuckin' GI Joe. I got what da fuck it takes to be a soldier. Papa said so," Mekhi replied, confidently.

"Over my dead body," Karma replied with the raise of a brow.

"Ma—" Mekhi began.

"You're not going anywhere near the military," Karma explained through tight lips.

"I am, Ma. Whether you like it or not," Mekhi stated calmly.

Karma lunged at him, but Stuff blocked her from making contact. "Your grandfather abandoned his family behind that hoo-rah shit," she seethed.

"Sis," Stuff begged, wrapping his arms around her waist.

"My mother lost her life because of him! Because the Army owned his black ass, and he wasn't man enough to break free! He could have saved her! He was supposed to save her!" Karma screamed, with tears in her eyes.

Mekhi knew very little about his grandmother. There were photographs of her around the house. Oil paintings of her likeness hung in both restaurants and the crisis center. And he heard stories about how sweet she was through Maggie and Indigo. But anything else, he knew nothing. He never knew how she died and always wondered. But discussion about her demise was off limits. No one in the family ever spoke about that.

"Sis," Stuff repeated, holding her closer now.

"Save her from what, Ma?" Mekhi asked, in quiet caution.

Karma locked eyes with him, then looked away quickly. "You're not enlisting." She sniffled. "That's it. Let me go." She nudged Stuff.

Stuff did as he was asked.

"Save her from what, Unc'?" Mekhi inquired, looking to his uncle for a definitive answer.

Stuff shook his head in response, then walked away.

Chapter 8

"Hey, Rich!" Money called to his co-worker.

"What's up, man?" Richard shouted from the prep room.

"What was it that you wanted to ask me?" Money replied as he lay a variety of cheeses and meats down in the display case of the delicatessen section of the West Orange Shoprite.

"Oh, yeah. Thanks for remindin' me. I wanted to ask what'cha got planned for Thanksgivin'?" Richard walked out of the prep room and placed four more blocks of meat down on the counter.

Money rolled the sleeves on his chef's coat up and smiled embarrassingly. "Not much, Rich," he admitted. "I'll probably stop by Greater Harvest or St. James for a decent meal. Go back to the Y and read or watch TV, man."

Richard looked over at Money with furrowed brows. He was a heavy-set, white man with a long ponytail, well-trimmed goatee and sleeve tattoos. A biker who loved Jazz music and black women. His wife was a black woman. Richard liked Money very much. Even though the former officer had only been working beside him as a deli clerk for a little over three weeks, he admired his humility. He knew what he'd done, because he watched the news daily, but who was he to judge? Richard was a heroin addict who had been clean for sixteen years and counting. He'd hurt a lot of people along his messy journey, so Money's past didn't matter, nor bother him. As long as his partner learned from his mistake and didn't repeat it, all was good.

"What kind of way is that to spend your first Thanksgivin' out of the clinker?" Richard inquired sincerely.

"It's not like I have a lot of options." Money laughed.

"Havin' dinner with me and Sue is an option," Richard responded.

"Oh, no, I couldn't—"

"Why not?" Richard placed a hair net over his head.

"I just don't want to impose." Money placed his cap on his head.

"It's not an imposition when an invitation's been extended," Richard said.

Money shifted his weight as he and Richard placed plastic gloves on their hands. "I hear you, but—" Money countered warily.

"Now, now, don't get me wrong. I'm sure the food those nice folks at those churches are gonna be servin' is gonna be out of sight. But you don't need to be in that type of environment on a day like that. Around people—"

"Who are homeless like me?" Money smirked.

"All right, okay. Yeah, if you want to put it like that."

Richard shrugged.

Money shook his head, laughing to himself.

"I'm just sayin', I've been where you are. When you get your plate of food, sit down and get ready to dive in, something stops you and tells you to take a look around. So, you do. And it's in that moment when you realize you're sittin' in a hall with other men, women, and children of all ages, backgrounds, cultures, and stories. Everyone is hungry, everyone is filthy, everyone has fallen on bad times or bad luck or bad decisions. It's depressin'. And if you experience it enough and finally get tired of it, you make a vow to change yourself and your life for the better. You keep that vow and never step foot in that place again. You never look back, my friend. Okay, so, those church kitchens are open for you. Well, so is my wife's," Richard responded honestly.

The two men locked eyes. Richard raised his brow and smiled.

"Have you even talked this over with Sue yet?" Money asked.

"Whose idea do you think it is to have you over?" Richard hinted.

Money blushed.

"Come on, man. Don't make this big ol' bad country boy beg, now," Richard teased. He poked his bottom lip out and changed the expression on his jubilant face to a sad one.

Money fought the urge to smile, but succumbed to it. "All right, all right," he surrendered.

"That's my man," Richard said, patting Money on his back. He walked to the prep room to retrieve a box of wax paper.

Money completed his inventory check and looked up to see a woman wearing a gray sweat suit and running sneakers waiting to be assisted. But her back was turned to him as she took a glance at the shopping list in her hand.

"My apologies for the wait, ma'am. What can I get for you this morning?" he asked once he spotted the white ticket in her left hand.

The woman turned and set her eyes on the face from which the kind, raspy voice had come. Her appreciative smile quickly faded. Time stood still.

"Karma?" Money queried, squinting.

Money's heart raced. He slowly slid the cap off his head and clutched it between his muscled hands. He'd played this moment over and over in his head, every day for the past three weeks. Now here she was, standing before him . . . older, radiant, scared and speechless.

"How have you been?" Money asked, trying to break the silence between them.

"I've . . . been better," she mustered.

"I can dig it." He grinned sweetly. "How are the kids? Your dad?"

"My father . . . died, um, three weeks ago," Karma informed him.

"Oh. I'm-I'm so sorry, Karm," Money professed. "I know how much you loved him."

"Thank you," she replied, with tears in her eyes.

"And the kids?" Money pried.

Karma shook her head and smiled nervously. "I can't—
"

"No, no, you're right. I know. I'm sorry." He held his hands up, surrendering. Money knew better than to ask her about the kids. The kids were off limits . . . well, Mekhi was. Technically, he could see and speak to Mimi. She was over eighteen years of age, but he knew Karma would never divulge her whereabouts. And Mekhi . . . Mekhi, unfortunately, was still a minor and still a victim of a horrific crime—*his* victim and *his* crime.

"What can I get for you?" he continued.

"Where are you staying?" Karma asked.

"The Y on MLK Boulevard."

"Oh." Karma nodded slowly.

"Temporarily, of course. Until I save enough money to get a place of my own." Money tried to save face.

"Of course."

"You still on Highland Ave?" Money inquired with raised brows.

"No, but I'm still in Essex County," she admitted.

No way in hell was she going to tell this man where she currently resided. Mekhi didn't know his father was out, and as far as Karma knew, no one else in the family did either. She hadn't figured out how she was going to break the news to everyone, *if* she was going to break it to them at all.

"Oh, okay. Cool," he replied disappointingly .

A loud silence ensued.

Richard emerged from the back room and took his place on the other side of the deli. He noticed the loud silence between his friend and the attractive blonde dressed in sweats.

"Well, I guess I'll give you my order now," Karma said, breaking the silence.

"Shoot," Money responded.

"Uh, I'd like a half pound of Land O'Lakes yellow American cheese and a half pound of Schick's beef bologna, please," she requested with a small smile.

"Coming right up." He smiled.

Karma looked over at the overweight white man staring at her from behind the surface grinding machine.

"Hello," she said warily.

"Mornin', ma'am," Richard greeted with a smile.

"Here you go." Money extended his full hand to his lost love.

Karma carefully took the contents from his gloved hand and nodded appreciatively. "Thank you."

"My pleasure," Money replied, trying to evoke a look of adoration from her.

Karma quickly looked away. She placed her cold cuts in her cart and sashayed away.

"Karm! Karm!" Money yelled after her.

She stopped and turned back in his direction.

"Can we get together sometime?" he asked with hopeful eyes. "Catch up?"

"Oh, I don't think that's a good idea," she replied honestly.

"I just want to talk to you."

"I don't know, Money."

"Please? I just want to talk. Nothing more, nothing less."

"I'll think about it."

"Okay. Okay." He smiled.

"She didn't say *no*," Money said to himself.

Karma returned the smile before sauntering away.

Money and Richard followed her with their eyes until she was completely out of sight.

"Who was that fox?" Richard asked.

Money licked his lips, and then pursed them.

"That was *her*."

Chapter 9

Mekhi rested his arms against the edge of the pool, waiting for Father Doherty, the assistant coach, to relay his time. The 50-meter freestyle was his specialty, a race that was only twenty-one seconds in time. Mekhi wiped his face with his hand as he looked up at the casually dressed, freckle-faced man.

"Twenty-one-forty-three, Parks," Father Doherty said, looking down at his stopwatch.

"Damn," Mekhi grumbled, slapping the water in frustration.

"What was that, son?" Father Doherty asked, wanting to know if he heard Mekhi correctly.

"Nothin', Father," Mekhi huffed as he climbed out of the pool and made his way over to Carmine. He threw his best buddy a towel. Mekhi wiped himself with it, before taking a seat on the bench.

"Fuck!" Mekhi grumbled.

"Don't sweat it," Carmine said.

"How can you sit here and say dat, dude?" Mekhi asked, his elbows resting on his lap.

"Because you've been out of the water for a couple of

weeks, man. *I* expected it," Carmine replied.

"Well, I didn't expect dat shit. Dat shit right there was horrible," Mekhi exclaimed. Carmine patted Mekhi on the back.

"You were off by three seconds. So what! You're back now. You know what you have to do, so do it," he stressed.

"I know, I know." Mekhi sighed.

"Okay, then." Carmine smiled. "Ay, you think your mom's gonna let you stay late tonight? Practice the relay?"

"Yeah, she's got extra coverage."

"Cool." Carmine nodded. "Oh, wait, what about the party at The Strip?"

"What about it?" Mekhi quizzed.

"Does she know about it?" Carmine questioned.

"Yeah, she knows," Mekhi lied.

Karma had been keeping him on a short leash since the fight at the restaurant. Even though all was calm between them, it was only a matter of time before something would set either of them off, and the duo would be on the outs again.

"You sure?" Carmine asked in uncertainty.

"Ay, yo, what's wit' all da fuckin' questions, C, man?" Mekhi asked. "Can't you see I'm strugglin' right now?"

"Ay, look, I'm just makin' sure I'm not gonna get caught up in no shit tonight," Carmine admitted with raised brows and wide, serious eyes. "Every time we go to the Treat or The Strip, we end up fightin' some goons, then get dropped off at your mom's house by 5-0, man. The rest of the night, I'm keepin' you and her from killin' each other. I don't even get to sleep!"

Mekhi burst into laughter.

"It's not funny, bro," Carmine expressed sternly. "I hate gettin' in the middle of you and your mom's shit. You get mad disrespectful, makin' her cry and shit. I don't like it. I can't take it."

Carmine's words wiped the smile right off Mekhi's face. He was right. Trouble followed Mekhi wherever he went, and Carmine was always there to help him fight his battles, those with strangers or the ones with his mother. Right or wrong, invoked or provoked, Carmine was there—always.

"Ain't gonna be none of dat tonight," Mekhi assured him.

"I'm serious, dude," Carmine said warily.

"So am I," Mekhi countered. "Niggas leave me be, we won't have any trouble."

Mekhi stepped onto Martin Luther King, Jr. Boulevard, placing his wool skully on his head and Beats headphones over his ears. Father Doherty had given them a thirty minute break to eat. Carmine had caught a horrific cramp in one of his legs that the coaches were tending to. So Mekhi decided to venture off to the closest eatery to have dinner. He placed his hands in the pockets of his hooded sweatshirt and bopped his head to the sounds of Jersey's own, Fetty Wap. As he walked past the entrance of Arts High, he wondered if Ekua was inside. He'd been thinking about her since the game. Her cool, calm, and collected nature intrigued him. And even though he was still dealing with the loss of his grandfather and the stew of emotions within, Mekhi believed there was room to fit his hopes of something special with Ekua there.

Ekua walked out of the performing arts building, zipping her fitted waist-high Parka up. She hated the cold. The temperatures in North Carolina, where she was originally from, never plummeted like they did in Jersey. She couldn't wait to return south for college. She didn't know what university she wanted to attend, but she was absolutely sure that it was going to be an HBCU. Ekua retrieved her cell phone from her coat pocket and checked the time on its clock. Her mother was late picking her up again. The woman never arrived anywhere on time. Ekua chuckled to herself. It was too cold to stand outside and wait for her. And she didn't want to go back into the school. So she decided to take a walk. Indecisive of where she wanted to go exactly, she looked toward Springfield Avenue, then in the opposite direction where she spotted Mekhi walking past St. Matthews AME Church. She knew him anywhere. His limped-walk was a dead giveaway. The way he moved was almost like that of a tap dancer. He stepped with his left foot and dragged his right a bit, creating a rhythm all his own. His body rocked some as he stepped and dragged, reminiscent of a tree swaying in the wind. He always kept his head raised, chin up, eyes forward and shoulders squared like a king from their ancestral past. She loved it. He had the smoothest walk ever. Desi described it as a "pimp walk from one of those classic black 70s films, " but to Ekua, it was so much more than that. And she wanted to know where it came from. She took a deep breath in, then exhaled before jogging in his direction. She tapped him on his arm once she finally reached him.

Mekhi looked down and smiled coolly at the sight of Ekua. He removed his headphones from his ears, resting them around his neck.

"Hey." He nodded.

"Hey." She smiled. "Where you goin'?"

"Subway. Gotta thirty minute dinner break. What about you? What you doin' out here? It's mad dark."

"I had dance rehearsal. My mom's supposed to pick me up, but she's running late."

"Oh, aiight." Mekhi nodded again. "Want me to wait wit'chu—until she comes?"

"You don't have to." Ekua smiled in spite of herself. "She's always late. I'll be okay. Really. I'm covered. Besides, you have to eat."

"Nah, dinner can wait. I don't feel comfortable leavin' you out here by ya'self. It's too dangerous. I couldn't live wit' myself if somethin' happened to you while I was at Subway stuffin' my face."

Ekua and Mekhi locked eyes. There was so much sincerity behind his soft gaze.

"Okay," she said quietly.

The two began to walk back toward the school.

"So . . . how have you been?" Ekua asked, breaking the awkwardness between them.

"Aiight, I guess." Mekhi shrugged. "Got a lotta shit—I mean, *stuff* goin' on." He blushed in embarrassment.

"Like what?" Ekua smiled sweetly, looking up at him.

Mekhi looked down at Ekua, pondering if he should confide in her or not. She had such an innocent face. And her eyes. Those bedroom eyes were steady pulling him in. His mother always said the eyes were the windows to the soul. And Mekhi could see Ekua's soul was as pure as one could get.

"I got into a big fight wit' one of my boys last month," he began.

"The Puerto Rican one?" Ekua queried.

"Yeah," Mekhi replied as they stopped and settled in the entrance of the school. "How'd you know? Desi tell you?"

"Yeah." She nodded. "And I've seen you and your other two friends a couple of times after school, hanging out or whatever. And he'll walk right past you or cross the street."

"Word?"

"Did you . . . break his arm?" Ekua asked hesitantly.

Mekhi nodded shamefully. "I didn't mean to. And on top of dat, my moms had to pay his medical bills."

"Wow. Well, I guess the only bright side is bones heal.

Better than hearts most of the time," Ekua admitted, swaying from side to side against the evening autumn wind. "Do you think you two can fix it? Your friendship, I mean."

"I don't know." Mekhi shook his head. "He said some real foul shit. I mean— stuff. And you've seen how he's been actin' since it all went down."

"True." Ekua nodded. "I guess the real question is do you *want* to fix it?"

"Nah," Mekhi replied, matter-of-factly. "He ain't no friend. What he said was mad disrespectful and uncalled for. Stuff only a hater would say. And it ain't da first time. He's said some off da wall stuff ova da years. Rude and obnoxious stuff. Not only to me, but to C and Curt also. But we jus' thought he was playin' ''cause he joked around a lot."

"Well, maybe this was God's way of weeding your backyard," Ekua said.

"You were raised in da church, huh?" Mekhi grinned.

Ekua smiled in spite of herself. "How can you tell?"

"You talk about God a lot."

"Is that a problem?" Ekua asked with furrowed brows.

"Nah. Gotta believe in somethin'."

"We do." Ekua nodded. "Do you believe in God?"

"Sometimes," he confessed. "When things are goin' good."

"And when they're not?"

"I question Him." Mekhi stared straight ahead. "Curse

Him for allowin' my father to hurt me and my moms da way he did. For takin' both of my grandmothers away from me, especially my moms' mom, who I never gotta chance to meet. And my grandfather. What kinda God takes da people you need da most away?"

"The kind of God who needs them more," Ekua answered simply.

"Den he's a selfish muthafucka."

"And so are you."

Mekhi looked down at Ekua. Her regard was unwavering—face serious.

"He has His reasons, Mekhi. And instead of questioning and cursing Him for the losses in your life, you should thank Him and rejoice. You *had* them. You know what it means to be loved. What it *feels* like. There are people out here who have no one and will *never* know what it's like to love someone and have it reciprocated. If anything, you should be grateful."

For a moment Mekhi pondered over her declaration before looking back down at her. She was visibly perturbed by his admission. "I ain't mean to offend you. Like I said, I gotta lotta stuff goin' on right now." He sighed. "I wish I had your faith. Believed in somethin' like you do. It says a lot about you."

"Really? Like what?" Ekua queried with a slight attitude.

"It says, you're not like da rest of dese girls up here. I could tell from da first day we met, you were different. You walk different. You talk different. You're jus' different.

You didn't have to ask me how I was doin' after learnin' about my grandfather's illness. But you did. And I appreciate dat." He eyed her intensely. "Even tonight, you asked me how I was doin'."

"Because it's important . . . to me." Ekua blushed, casting her eyes to the ground.

"Why?" Mekhi asked.

"Because you always look sad or angry. And that's no way to be. No way to live."

"You're right." Mekhi nodded slowly. "I gotta do betta if I'm gonna be ya man. Right?" he asked, waiting for her to meet his gaze once again.

"Right." Ekua grinned, looking up at him.

Mekhi returned the smile, excited about what was to become of them.

Chapter 10

Did their love ever change? Karma thought as she stood in the entryway of the reception hall at *Afro-Cubana's* watching the elder couple cut into their four-tiered anniversary cake. The Calloways were celebrating their fiftieth year of blessed matrimony. The hall was filled with their adult children, grands and great-grands, cousins, nieces, nephews, friends and colleagues. Mr. and Mrs. Calloway were an attractive couple. He was tall and slender, while she was short and stocky. They complimented each other, not only in style of dress and stature, but in appearance and mannerisms. Karma's chances of ever experiencing any type of wedding anniversary were slim to none. Her days of wanting to be a bride died the night her mother was killed.

"*Me voy, querido*," Miguel said, walking up behind her.

Karma turned toward her uncle with worried eyes. "Are you all right?" she asked with concern. His hand was completely wrapped in gauze, his arm in a sling. Mekhi's altercation had done a number on his cooking hand. It had been cut down to the bone. Surgery ensued, like it had years ago with Karma. Only this time, the doctors were uncertain if he would ever regain full usage of it. Cooking was her uncle's passion. And now, his future in the kitchen looked bleak. Neither of them knew what he was going to do if those days were over.

"Oh, yeah, yeah. Everything is fine, *princessa*. I just have to leave a little early," he explained, putting his coat on. "But before I go, I want to talk to you about something."

"All right." Karma winced, crossing her arms.

"I went to the Shoprite in West Orange yesterday to get a few things. And I saw *loco loco* there." Miguel pursed his lips in disgust. "Did you know he was out? That he works there?"

"Yes." Karma nodded dejectedly.

"You're keeping secrets now? From *me?*" Miguel asked solemnly.

"No, *Tio*. Never." Karma shook her head vehemently. "I just . . . I saw him there also, a couple of weeks after we buried my father. There was a conversation, but it was brief. Very brief."

"Have you had any contact with him since then? At all?" Miguel asked, with the tilt of his head.

"No," Karma said calmly.

"Do you plan to?"

"No, *Tio*. No. Why? What's the matter?"

"We didn't succeed the last time. And that bothers me. But I can make sure we do *this* time," he stated stoically, his eyes bugged.

"No, *Tio*. He isn't worth it. I'd rather you let him live

and suffer. Be reminded everyday of what he did, than to take his life and give him peace."

"Okay. Okay." Miguel nodded against his better judgment. "But if—"

"No *ifs*.'" Karma shook her head. "No *ifs*."

"Okay." Miguel smirked. "Then, I'm off."

"Where?" Karma asked.

"*Tengo una fecha*," he exclaimed, showing off a pretty dentured smile.

"I'm sorry. What?" she asked in shock.

"A date," Miguel replied proudly.

"With who?" Karma folded her arms at her chest.

"Do you remember your mother's nurse? The one she had during her stay at St. Barnabas?"

"Can't say that I do. Mommy had so many nurses," Karma declared. Soleil had more stints in the hospital than she cared to remember.

"Well, Ms. Hanks—"

"Ooo, Ms. Hanks!"

"Yes, Ms. Hanks." He chuckled. "She was your mother's nurse during her hysterectomy recovery."

Karma sorted through her mental rolodex, trying to put a face with the name. "Wait, is she the tall one? She wore her hair in an afro and had glasses?"

"She's the one," Miguel confirmed.

"Aww, she was so nice, *Tio*." Karma gleamed.

"She still is."

"Mommy liked her very much."

"She did. Well, Ms. Hanks moved into my building a couple of days ago. I saw her in the lobby, asked her if she remembered me and she said yes. Now we are going out to dinner and a movie."

"Aww, that's great, *Tio*. I'm so happy for you." She hugged her favorite uncle tight.

As far back as Karma could remember, her uncle never had a female counterpart. He was a lone ranger. She figured he stayed by his lonesome because he didn't want to know his siblings' pain or their failure in love and successes in loss.

"Thank you, *mi vida*." Miguel blushed. "Are you going to be all right?"

"Of course I am," she replied, waving her hand dismissively. "Eddie and the boys are here. I'll be fine," she reassured him. "Go. Enjoy yourself."

"All right." Miguel secured his scarf around his neck.

"Please tell her I said hello."

"I will." Miguel patted his niece on her cheeks. "*Te amo.*"

"*Te amo, demasiado. Divertirse.*"

Miguel kissed her on the forehead, turned away, and then made his way out of the building.

"Hey, beautiful," a voice suddenly whispered into Karma's ear. Karma shivered under the touch of Hassan's soft, full lips. He wrapped his strong arms around her and kissed her on the neck thereafter. She smiled, placing her arms over his and settled in his loving embrace.

"What are you doing here? It's late."

"I told you I was coming," he reminded her. "You didn't believe me?"

"No, I didn't."

Hassan shook his head in playful disbelief. "You've got no faith in a brotha."

"Oh, please." She smirked.

"What time is this over?"

Karma looked down at her watch. "Midnight."

"Oh, so they've only got fifteen minutes left."

Karma looked back at him with furrowed brows. "Excited, are we?"

"Just a little But on a serious note, and uh, more importantly, how are you? Are you tired?"

"A little. Why?" Karma's brow rose.

"Because I want to take you somewhere."

"Tonight?" Karma searched his eyes for humor.

"Yeah. Is that a problem?"

"It depends." She signaled her staff to begin wrapping up the affair.

"On?" Hassan pried.

"Where you plan to take me," Karma said, looking up at her lover.

"Do you trust me?"

"Last time a man asked me that, I wound up pregnant," she admitted, laughing to herself.

"Well, those days are over for you, right? So, you're good."

"What!"

"What?" Hassan shrugged. "Haven't you gone through that change of life thing, or whatever it's called, already?"

"No, I have not!" she huffed. "You know I haven't!"

"I know. I'm just kidding, kidding . . . kiddinggg."

"Yeah, okay."

"I am." He laughed.

"I'll remember that the next time you want *special attention*," she jeered.

"Aww, don't do me like that, baby. Look, just to show you how sorry I am, I'll help you clean and close up. How's that sound?"

"Sounds like a desperate attempt to get back in my good graces." She walked out onto the celebration to service the Calloway family.

"Is it working?" Hassan called to her back.

"No," she replied over her shoulder.

Chapter 11

The benefits of the army were in no comparison to what the Olympics had to offer. The remainder of swim practice had gone well. Mekhi fell back into his groove, and thoughts of next year's trials began to take the place of his plans to enlist. He, along with the coaches and his teammates, were pleased with his performance. Now it was time to celebrate the small feat. The Strip was holding its annual Pre-Thanksgiving party, and the boys were ready to take it by storm. Their first order of business was to find the best cabana to stand in. It had to be large and have the best view of the crowd.

The Strip was a Las Vegas-style three-story nightclub located on North Center Street in Orange. The club featured five separate atmospheres, including three dance floors, one which rotated, private cabanas, VIP bottle service areas, and a sushi bar.

Mekhi, Curtis, and Carmine walked in dressed to the nines, greeting their colleagues from school and the neighborhood. They walked up a short flight of stairs and settled in an empty cabana adjacent to the stage. They acknowledged the DJ with nods as he spun a classic Jersey club record. Mekhi sat down in the cabana's booth, bobbing his head to the bumping bass. Curtis sat beside him, locking eyes with a number of potential conquests.

"Ay, Khi," he said, lightly backhanding him in the chest.

"Sup?" Mekhi replied.

"My bad for what went down at the bus stop a couple of weeks ago. I ain't mean no disrespect, nah mean? To you or Desi . . . *especially*, Desi."

"You good, man," Mekhi assured him. "It's deaded."

The two ended their dispute with their secret handshake.

"Cool, cool." Curtis nodded.

A moment of silence grew between them.

"So I mean, I'm kinda feelin' her."

"Who?" Mekhi asked, scouring the crowd for Ekua.

"Desi," he admitted.

"What?" Mekhi snapped.

"I'm feelin' her." Curtis shrugged.

Mekhi listened carefully. He said nothing.

"Would you be mad if I tried to holla at her?"

"Holla how?" Mekhi cut his eyes at his best friend.

"You know."

"No, I don't. Holla how? Holla like a tiger caught by his toe holla? Holla like a banshee holla or like . . ." Mekhi created a vagina with his hands.

"Come on, man. You know it ain't like that."

"I do? Really?" Mekhi remained expressionless.

"It ain't like that, man. I wouldn't do that to your cousin. She's . . . she's special."

"How da fuck you know she's special? You don't even know her," Mekhi growled.

"Well, I . . . I wanna get to know her . . . if you let me," Curtis replied.

Mekhi thought about it for a moment. Curtis had the worst reputation out of them all. He had, however, known him for a number of years now, and he'd rather Desi date one of his friends than some stranger who he would have to watch closely.

"Aiight, look. I'ma give you my blessin'. But if you fuck this up, hurt her in any way, I'ma fuck *you* up," Mekhi said, pointing his finger.

"Bet!" Curtis smiled as his eyes settled on the Latina who'd taken an interest in Mekhi at his basketball game. She was coming their way. "Ay, bruh, isn't that the chick who got into it wit' Desi at the Prudential Center?"

Mekhi followed Curtis' eyes and sighed heavily. "Hell yeah. Damn," he confirmed. "She betta not start no shit."

The Latina, dressed in a mini orange and white blouson skirt, stepped to the base of the cabana with her girlfriends in tow.

"Where's ol' girl at?" Latina asked, popping her wad of gum.

"You mean my cousin?" Mekhi smirked.

"Oh, she's your cousin?" she asked with genuine surprise.

"Word," he replied with his head tilted back.

"I didn't know that, *papi*. I thought she was a bitch you used to fuck wit' or whateva."

"Nah, she's fam."

"Oh, okay." Latina pursed her lips as she caught Carmine's eye.

"So, listen. She was wrong for puttin' her hands on you and callin' you out ya name," Mekhi began.

"Yeah, she was."

"And she knows dat. So whateva it is dat you and ya girls got planned for her tonight . . . dead it."

"And if I don't?" Latina smirked.

"Den my mans here won't fuck wit' you da way you want 'im to," Mekhi said with the raise of his brows.

Latina looked back and forth from Mekhi to Carmine. She noticed the cut in Carmine's brow. She liked it. And he was much more handsome than Mekhi.

"Okay. I got 'chu. You gon' be here for a while?" Latina asked, turning her attention to Carmine.

"All night, love." Carmine grinned.

"Good." She smiled back. "I'll be back then."

"You better." Carmine watched her disappear into the crowd. "I'ma bag her in the bathroom. Gimme an hour," he whispered in Mekhi's ear.

"Do you, fam." Mekhi shrugged nonchalantly.

"She's here. How's my hair? Does it look okay? " Curtis asked Mekhi and Carmine as he watched Desi and

Ekua enter the club.

"How's my breath?" He blew his cool breath in Mekhi's face.

"Ay yo, get da fuck outta here, man!" he replied, shoving him.

Desi and Ekua danced through the crowd, approaching the boys with wide smiles and innocent eyes.

"Heyyy," they sang.

"What's up?" Carmine replied, smiling back.

"What's good wit'chu?" Curtis added, smiling harder. He and Desi's eyes met and held as the girls ascended the stairs.

"What y'a'll doin' wit' ya stomachs out like dat?" Mekhi snorted . Both girls were dressed in Urban Outfitters crop tops—their stomachs cut in fourths and sixths.

"It's the style, *primo*," Desi beamed. "You no like?" she teased. Desi wore fitted jeans, a knitted fingerless glove on one hand, and high-heeled Timberland boots. Her thick mane was styled in a mid-high ponytail, making her big hoop earrings visible.

"Nah," he replied with a half-smirk.

"Well, I do," Curtis confessed.

Mekhi snapped his head in Curtis' direction, and he gave him a wary glance. Curtis, in turn, held his hands up in submission.

"I'm jus' sayin'. They look good."

"They do." Carmine nodded. "Not trashy at all."

"Thank you, C. Curtis." Desi and Ekua grinned as Desi twirled.

Carmine nudged Mekhi thereafter. "Lighten up, bro."

Mekhi shook his head in disgust.

"So, who's gonna be my dance partner tonight?" Desi asked, winding her hips.

"Well, it's not gonna be me," Carmine confessed. "I don't dance."

"What are you afraid of, C? I mean, your hair is glued in place. You're Sicilian, which practically makes you a nigga since Africa is across the way. So, what's the problem?" Desi badgered with a grin.

"Wooow," Curtis sang with raised eyebrows.

He and Mekhi burst into laughter. "She's gotta point, bruh," Mekhi confirmed.

"Man, shut up." Carmine smirked, shoving Mekhi playfully. "I just don't dance, Des."

"Okay, okay." Desi chuckled. "What about you, Curtis? You gonna punk out like C?"

"I may be a lot of things, Red. But a punk, I'm not." He smiled as he took her hand and led her to the dance floor.

"You upset?" Ekua asked, slowly walking toward Mekhi in baggy cargo pants, bangles on both arms, and high-heeled sneaker boots. She modeled a fresh doobie, which she knew would be sweated out by the end of the night. Her side tresses rested at her shoulders and the oversized hoop earrings swung with each shift of her head.

"A little," Mekhi replied with the tilt of his head.

"I didn't know you were so conservative."

"About certain things. Yeah." He gave her a once-over.

"Good to know." Ekua smiled, reeking up the seriousness between them. "I'll make sure I stay close to you tonight, then."

"You do dat." Mekhi smiled in spite of himself. He watched her beautiful red undertone emerge to the surface of her cocoa-toned skin.

Across the ballroom, Jamie watched Mekhi and Ekua get cozy on the couch in their cabana. He'd parted ways with the crew after the brawl at the restaurant. He didn't like the way Carmine and Curtis put cleaning and restoration before his need of aiding. And he especially didn't like Mekhi for breaking his throwing arm, and now, his ego. His dream of playing college and professional baseball was deferred. His arm was shattered beyond repair. And his dream of courting and bedding Ekua, the same. He'd laid eyes on her first. Mekhi didn't even want to have anything to do with her. He'd shown no interest. Now suddenly, they were locked arm-in-arm, engulfed in deep conversation on the other side of the room. Jamie swore that he would make Mekhi pay for destroying his life. One way or another.

"What it do, Roberto Clemente?" a tall, Latino male dressed in all yellow yelled gleefully.

Jamie turned toward the voice as the person approached him. Juan Hernandez was a young Puerto Rican thug from

Jamie's neighborhood. The two played Pop Warner football and baseball together as children. He, however, unlike the baseball star, was from a broken home. He was the oldest of eight and his mother had forced the roles of father and provider on him at the age of ten. In search of the love and security he wasn't receiving at home, he found it within the arms of the South Ward Yellow Jackets. Robbing, killing, and dealing drugs were as easy as breathing for him. He wasn't a leader yet, but he was close. And he always looked out for his family—those in his home, within his set, and Jamie.

"Hey, Pa-Pa." Jamie smiled, never taking his eyes off the couple.

"I ain't seent chu in a minute. What chu been up to?" Juan asked.

"Shit. Goin' to school. Playin' ball. Well . . ."

"What da fuck is ya arm doin' in a cast, *cabrone*?"

"Dat *maricon* ova dere in da MGM cabana broke it."

"*Papi* in da cream sweater?" Juan squinted.

"Yeah."

"I thought dat was ya boy," Juan said, placing his hands in his pocket. He studied Mekhi long and hard.

"*Was. Dat hijo de la gran puta* ain't shit to me now."

"You can't play no more?"

"No." Jamie's eyes filled with tears.

"So, wha'chu gonna do wit' ya' self now?"

"Probably drop out. See what dat Yellow Jackets life be about." He eyed his childhood friend.

"It's about time, *papi*." Juan smiled widely as he slapped hands with Jamie. "I got'chu. I'ma teach you everything I know."

"Cool." Jamie nodded.

"But first thing's first." Juan snickered as he watched Mekhi and Ekua embrace in a sweet kiss.

Chapter 12

Karma stood before the Central Park carousel with her mouth agape. The sight was absolutely spectacular. Its sweet calliope music played as fifty-seven horses spun around, falling and rising to its melodic sounds. She turned to tell Hassan how beautiful the attraction was, but his positioning threw her completely off-guard.

"Will you marry me?" Hassan asked, kneeling on one knee.

"What?" Karma asked, in total shock. She looked over at the coachman, then back down at Hassan.

"Will you be my wife?" he asked again, opening a small, square box that housed a brilliant two-carat cushion-cut halo diamond engagement ring.

Once again, Karma's mouth fell open. She thought their little trip to the city was a random, yet romantic one. They'd driven over in Hassan's Infiniti QX80, settling at 64th Street, where they were greeted by a coachman named Steven and his horse Midnight. Hassan assisted her into the covered coach where a bouquet of red roses and a box of chocolates lay in waiting for her. Karma smiled, taking the items into her arms and sitting down on the velvet-covered seat. She and Hassan quickly buried themselves under the extraordinarily plush blanket and into the park on a late-night escapade. Steven made sure they saw the main sites on the tour: The Wollman Rink, the Pond, the Central Park Zoo, Sheep Meadow, the Mall, the Dakota and lastly, the carousel.

"I—" Karma began.

"Before you answer, I just want to say this: I know the way we got together was unusual. Many would say it was unprofessional . . . on my part. But you know I beg to differ," he stated, staring her squarely in the eyes. "I know you don't like sneaking around and keeping *this* from Mekhi—or the rest of your family."

Karma quailed when he said Mekhi's name. He would surely lose his mind if she accepted this man's proposal. Mekhi despised Hassan. Any teenage boy would. Karma couldn't give him her hand. She and Mekhi's relationship would forever be severed if she did.

"But I love you. I can't help it, I can't shake it . . . and I don't want to," Hassan confessed. "I know you love me just the same, which makes it painful for you, I know. But I don't want to hide anymore."

Karma slowly shook her head from side-to-side. "I can't," she whispered. "I can't sacrifice my relationship with my son. We've hurt him so much as it is. I don't think—"

Hassan nodded understandably. "What if I asked him for his blessing?"

"You forget, I have two children," Karma said with the raise of her brow.

"Then I'll ask them both. Mimi will be here for the holidays, won't she? So I'll ask them then," Hassan confirmed.

"He's not going to give it to you, baby," Karma replied, shaking her head.

"Maybe, maybe not. All I can do is try, right?" He grinned, standing to his feet. He snapped the box shut, then placed it back in his trench coat pocket. "Come on, let's get you back." He took her hand into his and led her back to the horse and carriage.

"Baby." Karma sniffled, looking up into his deep brown eyes.

"You don't have to say anything. I got this," he assured her with a long kiss on her needing lips.

The couple settled back under the warm coverlet, closing their eyes and allowing the trotting of Midnight's hooves to steal them away.

Karma's phone vibrated in her purse, waking her out of her light slumber. She retrieved it and winced at the UNKNOWN title displayed across the screen.

"Hello?" she said into the receiver.

"You have a collect call from—" the operator stated.

"Mekhi," he said in the absence of her tone.

"Do you accept the charges?" the operator asked.

"Yes," Karma replied, abruptly sitting up.

"Please hold," the representative countered.

Hassan awakened from his nap and looked over at Karma in curiosity. "You al—" he began, before she held her hand up, silencing him.

"Ma?" Mekhi said hesitantly.

"Mekhi, you better not be callin' me from the county," she threatened.

Silence responded to her threat.

"Hello?" Karma spat.

"Yeah," he answered.

"What the fuck are you doin' down there?"

"Fightin'."

"Fighting who? You were supposed to go straight home after school and stay there!"

"I know. But dere was a party at The Strip. So I went. And den dese Newark niggas came at me from outta nowhere and we got into it."

Karma's chest tightened and ached. She rubbed it as she tried to control her emotions. "Well, what exactly do you want me to do, Mekhi? It's . . ." Karma looked down at her watch. "Three-thirty in the damn morning—*Saturday* morning at that! I don't know, I just . . . you're gonna have to sit there until Monday."

"I know. I just . . . I just wanted to tell you where I am," he said grimly.

Karma choked back a set of tears.

"Bye." He ended the call.

She closed her eyes, gripping her phone in her gloved

hand. A river of tears began to fall, staining her flushed cheeks. She'd almost grown accustomed to Mekhi's calls from the county jail . . . *Almost.* But for some reason she thought that he'd finally mellowed out and gotten back on the straight and narrow path. She felt so stupid to have had such hope. He would probably never get himself together. She had to accept it. She *needed* to accept it. He was going to blame being fatherless for his misbehavior. He was going to blame *her* for the rest of his life. Karma didn't know what to do. Hassan took her into his arms, as he'd done so many a night, and held her close.

"He's going to be the death of me," she cried.

Chapter 13

"Yo, I told that nigga to just walk away, man," Curtis explained as he, Carmine, and Ekua stepped out of the metal detector in the foyer of the Essex County Courthouse.

"We all did," Carmine added, following suit.

Carmine pressed the UP arrow on the wall between elevators 1 and 2. Elevator 2's bell chimed and its doors opened. The trio made their way inside.

"I'm tired of this dumb shit, man. Every time we turn around, Khi's locked the fuck up in this bitch," Carmine uttered.

"This isn't his first time?" Ekua asked, guardedly.

"Not even close," Curtis replied. "This is like his second home. He's been in and out of this joint for the past two years."

Carmine nudged him roughly in the arm.

"What?" Curtis asked obliviously. "Look, I woulda taken the L for 'im, but I don't jail. I got too much at stake to fuck around and do that shit, nah mean?"

"We all do, Curt," Carmine corrected him tersely.

"You're right, but—" Curtis continued.

"But what, man?" Carmine asked, interrupting him.

"Shit, I don't know. I mean, I told that fool the moment we got into the club, *no fighting*," Curtis stressed. "And who the fuck hauls off and spits in a pig's face?"

"Khi does," Carmine chimed, shaking his head.

"They could have killed him for doing that," Ekua said, just above a whisper.

The boys nodded in agreement.

"And who the fuck was the dude who started the fight anyway?" Curtis asked.

"I don't know," Carmine replied. "But I thought I saw Jamie in the crowd watchin' the shit go down."

Curtis cut his eyes knowingly at Carmine as the elevator stopped on their selected floor. The door slid open and the three of them walked off. They walked down a long corridor in search of their best friend's mother.

"Me, too," he said to Carmine. "Anyway, I ain't neva seen 'im before."

"Neither have I," Carmine added.

"Had a lotta yellow and black on, though," Curtis informed him. "I peeped *that* shit."

"Word. The only reason why his set ain't jump Khi was 'cause the whole damn hood was there. That bitch was outnumbered," Carmine informed Curtis.

"This shit is fucked up," Curtis sneered.

"You know he's gonna be gunnin' for him now, right?" Carmine uttered in a whisper.

"What does that mean?" Ekua asked, fearful of Mekhi's safety and her own.

"It means, you need to be careful when you're with Khi, Ekua," Carmine informed her. "Or reconsider your relationship with him if you don't wanna get hurt."

"Yeah." Curtis nodded as they turned a corner. "Bullets don't have names on 'em. And they don't always hit their intended target."

"But he didn't do anything. He didn't even know that boy," Ekua stressed, her voice high with worry.

"Doesn't matter," Carmine expressed.

The group immediately spotted Karma in the crowd of waiting citizens. She appeared to be in a deep conversation with a short, silver-haired white man.

Carmine stopped in his tracks.

"We need to tell his mother," Ekua proclaimed.

"No, we'll handle it," Carmine replied calmly. "She's got enough to worry about."

"Yeah," Curtis added.

"All right, well, listen . . . I-I-I gotta go," Ekua stuttered.

"Where?" Curtis asked in confusion.

"I just . . . I have to go." She back-stepped. "Please tell Mekhi I'm sorry."

"Ekua!" Curtis yelled at her back. "Ekua!"

Carmine and Curtis looked at each other, second-guessing themselves. Maybe they shouldn't have been so honest with her about their friend's rap sheet and head bounty. In their minds, they were protecting her. The last thing they wanted to do was scare her away.

Chapter 14

"I've neva met anyone like her before," Mekhi admitted. "She . . . she sees da good in me."

Karma stared straight ahead, her hands resting at nine and three o'clock on the steering wheel.

"Say somethin', Ma . . . please." ," Mekhi begged as his mother pulled into their driveway and parked.

"Don't ruin her," she said coldly.

"Why couldn't you say somethin' else? Why can't you believe in me like she does?" Mekhi winced. "I'm not gonna ruin her. I'm gonna do betta, Ma. I promise."

"Don't make promises you can't keep," she said dejectedly, cutting her eyes at him.

"Ma—" Mekhi began.

"*And* . . . if this girl is someone you can see yourself with for a long time, marry even, then you need to let go of your grandfather's dream of going into the Army," Karma noted seriously.

"It's not jus' his—" Mekhi began again.

"My mother spent the majority of her marriage raising me, alone," Karma professed, her eyes on the gazebo. "Is that what you want for this little girl if she should become your wife? If not, then you really need to think about what it is that you want. From her, from yourself, and most importantly, *for* yourself. Because I'm tired, Mekhi. I'm doing the best I can as your mother, but . . . I guess . . . my best isn't good enough. I'm trying to do right by you. I really am. But I can't . . . do *this* anymore. I won't." Karma sniffled. She slowly turned toward her son, locking her hazel eyes with his. "If you get locked up again, I'm going to leave you in there. Then I'm going to make arrangements to send you away."

"Away?" Mekhi asked, fearfully.

"*Yes, away.*"

Mekhi sucked his teeth and shook his head in disbelief. His nostrils flared as his lips tightened. His mother was overreacting. He didn't start the fight, the other boy did. He was just defending himself. She was being totally unreasonable.

"Dis is some bullshit," he mumbled.

"What?" Karma retorted with furrowed brows.

"Nothin'."

"No, I think I heard you say this was some bullshit."

"It is." Mekhi slumped in his seat.

"You know what? You're right. You are absolutely right, Mekhi. This *is* some bullshit. I don't know what your fuckin' problem is, but you better fix it."

"It's *you!* You're my fuckin' problem! Why da fuck did you have to get knocked up by that crazy ass nigga? Why couldn't you fall for somebody normal? Huh? Why?" he bellowed, rocking the car with his rage. "I'm da only one out of my friends who doesn't have a fuckin' father! Do you know how dat feels? It fuckin' hurts, man! It hurts!"

Karma's mouth lay open as she drowned in her only born's raging waters.

"I'm fucked up, Ma! Here and here," ." Mekhi pointed to his head and heart. "I'm fucked up. And as bad as I wanna get right, I don't know if I'm eva goin' to. You should have aborted me when you had da fuckin' chance." He, unlocked his seatbelt, then exited the car.

"I called her twice already and sent her like five text messages." Mekhi sulked.

"Well, maybe she's busy," Desi guessed.

"Nah. She always gets back to me quick." Mekhi sighed. "She's avoidin' me. I know it."

"No, you don't." Desi sighed. "She could be out with her mom or something. Whatever. Look, that's the least of your worries. What you said to *Tia* was mean, *primo*.

"I know. I'm gonna go and apologize to her after I get off da phone wit' you," he replied as he ran his hand over his doo-rag.

"You need to do more than that. You better go and buy her some flowers or tickets to a show or something."

"Word," Mekhi agreed.

"I'm serious," she countered.

"I know. I will."

"Okay. Ohhh, wait! I forgot to ask you if Mimi's coming up for Thanksgiving."

"Yeah, she is." Mekhi smiled widely. "She's comin' up da day before and stayin' for two weeks. I can't wait, yo."

"Neither can I. She's been gone for like, nine months, right?" Desi asked.

"Yeah, give or take," Mekhi replied.

"That's going to be good for you and *Tia.*"

"Yeah, things are always better when she's home."

"Because she's the voice of reason."

"Yeah and so much more. She's . . . *everything.* Mimi knows how to talk to me, nah mean? She listens to what I have to say. She never judges me. I can talk to her about anything, like I can talk to you about anything. She never makes me feel less than, know what I'm sayin'?" Mekhi yawned.

"Yeah, I do." Desi empathized.

"I'm not sayin' my mother does, but it's jus' different wit' my sister."

The doorbell rang, interrupting Mekhi's thoughts. Whoever it was at the door was pressing the bell unremittingly.

"What da—" Mekhi said to himself.

"What's up?" Desi inquired.

"Somebody's ringin' da bell like dey ain't got no sense," he replied, jumping up from his bed. "Ma?" he called as he jogged out of his room and into the hallway. "Yo, I'll call you back."

"Okay," she responded, before ending the call.

"Ma?" Mekhi called again as he flew down the stairs to the front door. He unlocked the heavy wooden structure, then turned the knob.

"Where is she?" Hassan asked, storming into the foyer. "Karma?" he hollered.

"Yo, what da fuck you doin' here, man?" Mekhi growled.

"Where's your mother?" Hassan asked, scouring the rooms adjacent to the entrance hall.

"Yo!" Mekhi snarled.

"Karma?" Hassan yelled up toward the stairwell. He took a chance, running up toward the second floor. "Karma?" Hassan bellowed.

"Ay, yo! I'm talkin' to you, man!" Mekhi screamed to his back.

Hassan ignored him as he hurried to Karma's bedroom door. It was closed. He placed his hand on the knob and braced himself for the worst. When he opened it, Karma's body came into view. She lay on her side with her arms outstretched. Her hands were limp and an empty bottle of Tylenol lay on the floor beside the bed. A number of pills were scattered nearby. He ran over to her and turned her over onto her back.

"Karma?" he called, running his hand over her expressionless face. "Karma, baby, wake up," he begged softly.

Mekhi ran over to the bed, leaping onto it to get a closer

look at his mother's lifeless state.

"Mommy?" he said with wild eyes. He gently brushed her hair out of her face. "Mommy? Wake up."

"Call nine-one-one, Mekhi," Hassan instructed in a hushed tone.

"Mommy?" he said again, placing his hand on her still chest.

"Go, son. Go!" Hassan urged, lightly shoving him.

He began CPR as Mekhi scampered off the bed and flew out of the room. Mekhi sprinted down the stairs. He snatched the house phone from its cradle and with trembling hands, dialed the emergency number with his thumbs. He'd thought about using his cell phone, but remembered the reception in that area was horrible.

"Nine-one-one, what's your emergency?" the nasally speaking man asked on the other end of the line.

Chapter 15

Mimi walked hastily through the halls of St. Barnabas' psychiatric ward dressed in her military sweats. Her ship had come in two days ahead of schedule. When she stepped onto base, there was a message from Indigo waiting for her. Mimi thought it was unusual, so she immediately returned her call. *"Your mother tried to kill herself last night. She's in the hospital,"* were the only words Mimi comprehended during their exchange. She collapsed to the floor upon hearing the news of her mother's attempt on her life. Indigo filled her in on the text message Karma had sent Hassan, explaining Mekhi's recent arrest and his blackout in the car. She said she was tired of fighting a losing battle with him. She had no fight left in her and just wanted to go to sleep. Mimi took the earliest flight out of Virginia.

"There she is," Indigo stated to her mother and uncle.

The threesome met the frantic young woman midway, taking her into their arms and hugging her ever- so tightly.

"Where is she?" Mimi asked, handing her duffle bag to Miguel.

"In here," Indigo replied, gesturing to the room they were standing outside of.

The family stepped to the side, making a path for Mimi to walk along. She entered the room with measured steps, hoping . . . *praying* that when she pulled the curtain back, she would still be standing. She placed her hand on the drape and pushed it along its track. Her eyes settled on the woman who'd raised her as her own; she completely fell apart. The upper end of the bed was slightly erect. Karma was dressed in a hospital gown. Her hair was out, wild with curls. Her head was turned toward the window, her eyes closed, hands and feet strapped to the bars of the bed.

Indigo walked up behind Mimi, placing her hands on her back and shoulder. "I know, sweetie. I know," she expressed, her voice in a quiver.

"Why is she in restraints?" Mimi hiccupped.

"Because she's a danger to herself." Indigo sniffled.

Mimi wiped her face with her palm, and then the back of her hand. She slowly walked over to her mother, taking in the entire room. It was small, she thought. Not much light was coming in through the window. She turned her focus back to Karma and stroked her peaceful face. She appeared to have aged some since her last visit. Mimi had no idea of the weight in which her mother carried. She didn't know things had gotten much worse between her and Mekhi. When they spoke on the phone, she seldom complained about the restaurants or Mekhi's behavior. Mimi thought the two were finally in a place of contentment. How wrong she was.

She bent down and studied her mother's face more closely. New stress lines marked her forehead. Mimi took her fingertips and gently stroked her blonde and gray edges.

"I'm here, Mommy," she whispered into Karma's ear. "I'm home."

Mekhi flinched at the sound of the front door opening. He braced himself as Mimi entered their mother's home with her keys and duffle bag in hand. He listened closely to her steps as she closed the door behind her and threw the keys in the large ceramic bowl set atop an end table adjacent to the door. He was aware that his sister had spent hours at the hospital, talking to the doctors and nurses. Thanksgiving was two days away, and their mother would be spending it in that very place. Her 5150 was going to be lifted Friday and even then, the family was uncertain if she'd be released.

Out the corner of his eye, Mekhi watched Mimi step out of her sneakers and place them under the end table. He remained as she shuffled into the living room. Mekhi brought his knees to his chest as he pressed his back against the couch and continued playing 2K18. He never thought to pause the game to acknowledge her.

Steadily Mimi sat down on the couch beside her brother, retrieved the television remote from its cushion, and pressed the power button, shutting the electronic device off. She slowly leaned forward, resting her elbows in her lap and looked at their reflections in the black screen. Mekhi kept his eyes cast to the floor.

"Our mother . . . is strapped down to a bed . . . like an

animal," she hissed, her nostrils flaring. "An *animal*."

A loud silence befell.

"Why would you tell her she's to blame for your misery?"

Mekhi juggled the console in his hands.

"I asked you a question," Mimi sneered.

"I didn't mean it," he replied, tapping his foot.

"Yes, you did." Mimi begged to differ. "Try again," she said smugly.

Mekhi said nothing.

"You know, she can easily say the same about you," Mimi argued. "But she doesn't." Mekhi bit down on his bottom lip and shifted his weight. "That woman took me in and loved me and raised me as her own," Mimi seethed. "From the time I was four-years-old. My mother didn't want me! My mother didn't want any of her children! And that beautifully hard woman that we both call 'Mommy,' did," she stressed with tears in her eyes. "Do you remember when my biological mother died?"

Mekhi nodded.

"And I walked around here like I didn't care?" Mimi continued.

Again, Mekhi nodded.

"Well, I did. And Mommy knew that. She knew I was hurting and still carrying a heavy load of resentment toward her. And instead of telling me, *insisting*, that time would mend my heart, she told me to bury it with her. And that's what I did. We went to her wake . . . and I left it all there in that casket. Right along with her." Mimi nodded in remembrance. "If you want to be angry with someone, baby brother, be angry at Money Parks, our father. *He's* the one who put that gun to your back, not her."

"I am angry wit' him!" Mekhi said, slamming the controller onto the floor.

"Then you tell him that when you see him!" Mimi snapped. "Stop lashing out at *her!*"

"What?" Mekhi asked, perplexed.

"He's out," Mimi confessed. "Mommy told me in the last letter she wrote to me."

Mekhi turned and looked at his sister. Her cocoa-brown skin glowed. She smelled like vanilla and shea butter. Her hair was dread locked and styled into a fancy upsweep. They shared the same almond shaped eyes and full lips. Her nose was broader than his, and she had a small nose ring in her right nostril as well as in her left brow. Her baby fat was long gone as well as her interest in men. She loved women just as much as Mekhi did. Even though Evelyn had not understood it, Karma did and never questioned her. She only supported her and told her to be careful, as any loving mother would.

"How long has he been out?" Mekhi asked.

"About a month now," she said. "He works at the Shoprite in West Orange."

Mekhi rubbed his forehead in an attempt to comprehend the information he'd just obtained.

"Now, I am more than willing to make arrangements

for you to meet him while I'm home. That's if you want to," Mimi said.

"Mommy ain't gonna go for dat," Mekhi admitted in a small voice. "She ain't gonna allow it."

"Mommy doesn't have to know," Mimi replied directly. "But before we get there, you have to fix *here* first. Look at me," she ordered austerely.

Mekhi obliged without hesitation.

"We almost lost our mother last night because of you. *You*," she stressed, poking him in the forehead with her index finger. "And I'm telling you right now. If I ever— .. . *ever* get a phone call like that again, so help me God, Mekhi . . . I will make you disappear. Understand?"

"Yeah," Mekhi replied in a low voice.

Money walked out of the Shoprite behind the last minute Thanksgiving shoppers with bags of pie crust, sweet potatoes, bottles of vanilla and other ingredients inside. He didn't want to attend Richard's dinner without bringing a dish. So he decided he was going to make his mother's signature sweet potato pecan pie. He missed her dearly. She loved the holidays, especially Thanksgiving. Since her passing, it had become difficult to enjoy—to be grateful for anything. She was the only constant in his imprisoned life. The only one who visited faithfully and put money on his books, spoiled him rotten with care packages, handwritten letters and singing birthday cards. Then that all came to an end when age caught up to her, hindering her from making the trips anymore.

Money missed his mother so, and figured he always would. Her death was a blow to him, sending him over the edge once again. He lashed out and harmed two correctional officers as a result of it. Adding five more years to his ten-year sentence. But today he was free. And today he was grateful to have a friend like Richard because he hadn't made any at the halfway house since his release. He was going to walk into a home tomorrow. One full of warmth and love. And even though it wasn't his, it was one nonetheless.

As he walked toward his used 2008 Ford F-150, he thought about Karma and what she was doing at the moment. He thought about her every single day in prison and every day since his release. Money replayed their chance meeting two weeks ago over and over again in his head. He'd wanted to say more to her. Tell her how sorry he was for introducing her to misery, but his presence caused her to pause. Forced her to remember the pain that had been so unkind to her and their children. All Money wanted, was to be new company for her. Be the man he knew he could be for her and the father he never had for their children. Sixteen years. It sure was a long time to be locked away from them.

"Daddy," a sweet voice call in the distance. Money scanned the parking lot, finally setting his eyes on a cocoa-complexioned young woman who shared his eyes.

"Baby girl?" he sputtered, peering.

Mimi's lips spread into a broad smile. And before

Money knew it, she was running toward him and jumping into his arms. Tears fell from their eyes as they embraced long and hard. Money swung Mimi from side to side as she tightened her grip around his neck. Sixteen years. They hadn't seen or spoken to each other in sixteen years. Money wasn't allowed to have any photographs of Mimi or Mekhi as a result of his crime, so he created mental images of them based off the descriptions his mother gave him.

"Mmm, you feel so good in my arms," Money hummed in her ear.

"Daddy". Mimi sobbed. "I missed you so much."

"I missed you, too, baby girl." He sniffled. Money gently put her back down on the ground, then took her wet face into his cold, massive hands. "Let me look at you," he smiled, leaning back.

Mimi returned the smile while wiping her running nose with the back of her hand. "You're beautiful, baby," Money said proudly.

"Thank you." Mimi blushed.

"Come on. Let's hop into my truck and get warm," Money offered as he unlocked the truck with the press of a button.

"Okay." Mimi sniffled as she opened the passenger door and climbed into the cold vehicle.

Money shut the door and ran to the driver's side, jumping in. He placed the grocery bags in the backseat before sticking the key into the ignition and starting it up. He turned the heat on thereafter.

"Baby girl. What . . . what are you doing here?" he asked, taking all of her in.

"Mommy told me you were working here. So I thought I'd take a chance and see if you were here today." She grinned.

"I'm glad you did." Money returned the smile. "It's been a long time, baby girl. A long time."

He was so happy to hear that Karma thought enough of him to inform Mimi about his release and whereabouts. Maybe there was still hope.

"It has, Daddy," Mimi agreed painfully. "How are you?"

"I'm better, now that I've seen you," Money admitted. "Being out—being out here, back in society again is an adjustment."

"Do you need anything?" Mimi asked. "I can help you. Just tell me what you need."

"No, no. I'm good, baby girl." Money shook his head.

"You sure?" Mimi chimed.

"Yeah, I'm sure." He smiled. "Forget about me for a moment. How are *you* doing?"

"The Navy is treating me well."

"The Navy?" Money asked with raised brows.

The last time his mother spoke of Mimi was when she was a junior in high school.

"Yup. Enlisted right out of high school." She nodded. "I wasn't sure what I wanted to major in, or what school I wanted to attend for that matter. But I did know I wanted to travel the world. So, I talked to Mommy about backpacking around the world with some friends, but she was totally against that. Especially, since I had no job or money. So then I asked about her thoughts regarding my interest in the Navy. And she was against that as well."

"She's against all things military."

"And I understand why." Mimi sighed. "But after a week-long convo about it and meeting with a recruiter, she supported my decision to enlist. Been Navy for four years now. I love it."

"That's peace, baby." Money smiled widely. "I mean it. I'm proud of you. You gonna re-enlist?"

"Yeah, I am. Gonna apply for the officer program when I get back to the port. Make a career out of it."

"Damn. That's great, baby. I mean it. Your grandmother would be so proud of you."

"Thank you, Daddy." Mimi blushed again. "I miss her."

"Me too, baby. Me too." Money choked back tears. "The Navy's got you pretty busy. Are you dating? Do you have time to date?" he asked, clearing his throat.

"Yeah, I date from time to time. And I definitely have my eyes set on someone right now." Mimi smiled coyly.

"Oh, yeah?" Money grinned.

"Yeah." Mimi nodded slowly.

"What's his name?" Money asked excitedly.

"*Her* name is Vivian," Mimi replied, raising a sinister brow.

Money stared at her in sheer disbelief. He didn't recall

his mother ever mentioning that Mimi was a lesbian. Money began to rub his forehead. He looked out into the parking lot, then back at Mimi. *She doesn't look like a lesbian,* he thought. Then again, what did a lesbian look like?

"Daddy," Mimi said softly.

Money shook his head and continued to rub his brows.

"You being sick and locked up didn't make me this way. Lachelle being a drug addict didn't make me this way. God made me this way . . . and I love it. I'm happy."

Money studied the sincerity in her eyes. He didn't understand the LGBT culture. And being locked up for sixteen years with men who walked in heterosexual, then walked out homosexual didn't make sense to Money. He'd spent many a night listening to other men become victims of rape. Sheer terror and helplessness mixed with unadulterated masculine passion were sounds he would never forget for as long as he lived.

"Does your mother know?" Money asked, clearing his throat.

"Yes, she does. And she supports me 100%," Mimi confirmed proudly.

"Okay, okay. I need some time . . . to, uh—"

"I understand. We can talk about something else," Mimi offered.

"Okay, all right. Uh . . . how's your brother?"

Mimi looked away momentarily and sighed quietly, before meeting her father's soft gaze once again. "Not good."

Money shifted in his seat in discomfort. "No?" His brows knitted.

"No." Mimi shook her head. "He's doing wrong by Mommy. Causing her a lot of heartache and pain. She tried to commit suicide two nights ago."

"What!" Money leaned toward Mimi. He couldn't believe his ears. Just the thought of Karma entertaining the thought of suicide bothered Money. He couldn't imagine life without her. And he didn't want to.

"Yeah." Mimi sighed. "From what I was told, they got into an argument on the way home from court."

"Court?" Money asked in confusion.

"Yeah. See, Mekhi's been in and out of juvie for the last two years. Why? I don't know. But, anyway, they got into a really bad argument about you and Mommy's relationship. And he basically told her that she was to blame for his lack of self-control. And your absence."

Money sat back and looked away. He knew Mekhi possessed his temper from the moment he was born. That was the purpose of the attempt on his life. But since he survived, Money hoped that as Mekhi aged, the fury would subside over time. After hearing this news, he knew different.

"Mommy couldn't take it anymore. So she . . ."

"How is she?" Money was scared to ask.

"Tired," Mimi stated seriously. "She's not looking good, Daddy. Mekhi's really done a number on her. And with Papa gone and me not around to help keep him in check, she has her hands full."

"Your mother's strong," Money admitted. "She'll bounce back. That I can promise you. But your brother . . . where can I find him during the week?"

"He attends St. Benedict's," Mimi said. "He used to go to Orange High, but he got expelled his freshman year."

Money grunted and shook his head in discontent. It was time to show up and show out.

Chapter 16

Karma rubbed her sore wrists as she sat on the edge of her hospital bed. The restraints had left them tender and bruised, two painful reminders of her failed, desperate attempt to escape reality. She closed her eyes as her aunt ran her fingers along her scalp. It had been years since she'd braided her or Indigo's hair. Desiree allowed her to grease her scalp every two weeks, but nothing more.

"It be times like dis where me miss your mother de most. She could always count on I to do her hair, to keep it healthy and strong and styled beautifully. Me never tought me would outlive she . . . and Victor."

Karma squirmed at the sound of her uncle's name. Whenever he was the topic of conversation, her comfort level plateaued. After all, she tried to kill him years ago for raising his hand to her aunt. And even though her intentions were good, Maggie had her arrested and blamed her for the dissolution of their marriage, up until the day the man died. A heart attack. One minute they were enjoying their vacation at Walt Disney World with Indigo, Stuff, and Desiree, the next minute they were making funeral arrangements. Maggie moved in with Indigo quickly thereafter. Stuff and Desiree loved having her there. Not only did she cook and clean, but she spoiled them with more love and attention than Indigo could ever remember receiving. She kept them entertained with stories of her childhood and shared special memories of Soleil and Victor. Bringing excitement and the importance of grandparenthood into their home.

Maggie dipped her ancient finger into the jar of grease, placed it into her palm, and then rubbed her hands together. She took Karma's mane into her clutches and treated it with care.

"Me remember when your mother's hair was long like tis." She smiled. "You remember dat, gal?" Maggie brushed her hair.

"Mm-hmm, I do." Karma smiled.

"Her used to say your daddy loved it dat way. Him loved to pull it." She giggled.

Karma shook her head at the thought of her parents making love. "Is that why she cut it?"

"Dat is *exactly* why her cut it." Maggie chuckled. "Said him got a little carried away from time to time."

Karma shook her head again and sighed.

"A French-braid?" Maggie asked.

"Yes, please," Karma replied.

"Den a French-braid it is." She smiled.

"Thank you, *Tia*," Karma said over her shoulder.

"For?" Maggie inquired, parting her niece's hair.

"Taking care of me over the years. Forgiving me for what I did to *Tio*," she confessed softly.

"Forgiveness is de only true way of being free, baby," Maggie proclaimed. "If me didn't forgive you, me still would be a prisoner of hatred and contempt. Dat's no way to live. And me love you too much to hate you. Me loved your *mother* too much to ever hate you."

Karma leaned back into her aunt, falling into her loving embrace. Maggie squeezed her tightly as she placed a tender kiss on her cheek.

"Me love you," she proclaimed.

"I love you, too," Karma replied. She leaned forward and closed her eyes again. Maggie continued braiding her hair.

"Me hope dey have burners here for I to put de pans on," Maggie said.

"They should. Did you ask one of the nurses?" Karma implied.

"No, me didn't. Me will after I finish your hair."

"I would rather you all have dinner at home, *Tia*. This is no place to have Thanksgiving."

"And what makes you tink us care about your preference?" Maggie joked.

"*Tia*—"

"Us are spending Tanksgiving here wit' you and dat's final," Maggie said seriously. "Me don't want to hear another word about it."

"Okayyy." Karma sighed.

"Now, put your head down for I."

Karma did as she was told.

"Knock, knock," Hassan said, peeking his head in. He held a bouquet of flowers.

Maggie and Karma turned and smiled.

"Me am just finishing up," she said to him.

"No rush." He grinned.

"There," Maggie said, placing a small band on the end of Karma's braid. She briefly smoothed loose strands of blonde and gray hair down before gathering the jar of grease, comb, and brush. She placed the items in her tote bag before rising from the bed, patting Hassan on the arm and exiting the room.

"You look beautiful," he stated, approaching her.

"The lies you tell." Karma smirked, rising from the bed.

The two embraced in a long hug.

"Mmm, you smell so good," Karma said softly.

"I do it all for you, baby," Hassan admitted, gently lifting Karma's chin with his index finger and thumb. He studied the green specks around her irises, falling deeper into her hazel eyes. He licked his luscious lips, leaned down and met her mouth with his. They closed their eyes in unison, losing themselves in each other. Karma carefully took the bouquet out of his hand and slowly pulled away. She brushed her thumb against his pretty lips and smiled before kissing him once again.

"I love you, baby," Hassan confessed.

"I love you, too," Karma replied.

"Don't ever do anything like this again, okay?" he pleaded, with her face in his massive hands. "I can't bear the thought of losing you."

"I won't. I'm sorry."

"I'm just sayin', seventeen is too young to date," Stuff professed.

"Oh, my God, Daddy. You're being so unreasonable," Desi whined.

"Am I really?" Stuff smirked.

"*Yes*, you are," Desi replied. "I mean, you're acting like he never came to you and asked for your permission."

The Alonso-Davis clan gathered around a table in the dining hall of the hospital. They sat amongst other patients and their family members, nurses and other support staff, all of diverse backgrounds and cultures. Hassan and Karma stood in line, helping themselves to the endless dishes laid out on the rectangular table. Indigo, Stuff, Desiree, Maggie, Miguel and Ms. Hanks sat at their assigned table engaged in conversation and their overflowing plates.

"He did. And I told dat Jimmy Walker lookin' ass nigga *no*," Stuff

proclaimed, shoving a fork into his mouth.

"Who's Jimmy Walker?" Desi asked.

"Stuff," Indigo warned with a stiff eye.

"What?" he queried. "Look, no daughter of mine is goin' to date a snake like Curtis Jones III. He's a slick, fast-talkin', panty-droppin', no good piece of shit."

"Stuff," !" Maggie said, eyeing him.

"Sorry, Ma. Sorry," he apologized. "But I call 'em like I see 'em."

"Mommy?" Desi griped.

"We'll talk about it when we get home," Indigo stated as she took a sip of her punch.

"What's there to talk about? She's not datin' him, or anyone else for dat matter until she's forty," Stuff professed.

Karma and Hassan made their way back to the table and sat down.

"Mommy, you and Aunt Karma started dating when you were my age," Desi announced.

Karma looked up from her plate with wide, confused eyes.

"Those were different times," Indigo informed her. "Eat your dinner."

"I'm not even sexually active," Desi pronounced.

Stuff choked on the turkey and stuffing in his mouth.

"Desiree!" Maggie snapped.

Indigo patted her husband on the back, eyeing her daughter across the table with pursed lips.

"But I'm not, Nana," Desi confirmed.

"You better not be," Indigo jeered.

"What did she say?" Miguel asked the table as a whole.

"Nothing, honey. Nothing," Ms. Hanks lied.

Hassan scratched the back of his head while Karma took a sip of her soda.

"You okay?" Indigo asked Stuff. He nodded.

Indigo rose from the table, pointing her finger at Desiree and gesturing for her to get up and follow her out of the room. Desiree did as she was instructed. Mother and daughter stormed out of the room, brushing past Mimi and Mekhi.

Mimi bounced into the dining hall with Mekhi trailing behind. She spotted the family across the room and made her way over to them. They all stood to their feet and greeted her with hugs and kisses. She fell into Karma's arms and stayed there for some time. It felt good being in her strong arms again. She looked so much better today— healthier, happier . . . herself. Karma reintroduced her to Hassan. The two embraced and she proceeded to remove her coat. Hassan assisted her, and then placed it on the back of her chair. Mekhi watched the exchange between his sister, mother, and Hassan from the doorway. It was bad enough they were spending Thanksgiving in the hospital. The last thing he wanted was to spend it with the man who created division between his mother and him.

Karma looked toward the entryway and locked eyes with her son. His face was tight and his hands were buried in his coat pockets. His head was tilted back, and he was chewing gum. Karma sighed. It was now or never. She rose from the table, excusing herself. She maneuvered through the maze of tables and met Mekhi face-to-face.

"Are you going to join us?" she asked, breaking the awkwardness between them.

"Nah, I don't have much of an appetite," Mekhi replied, staring at Hassan.

Karma followed her son's gaze and nodded slowly. "Let's go to my room and talk," Karma suggested.

Mekhi looked down at his mother before backing out of the corridor and following her to her room. Karma walked to the window, crossing her arms at her chest.

"You're wondering why he's here," she stated. "Yes?"

Mekhi remained silent. Karma looked back at him for a brief moment, then faced the window once again.

"Well, we've been seeing each other—we never stopped seeing each other after *that day*," she confessed. "We love each other, Mekhi," she admitted, turning back to face him. "And he wants to marry me. But he won't ask for my hand until he has you and your sister's blessing."

"Fuck him!" Mekhi spat.

"That's what I thought you'd say." Karma grinned.

"I'm not givin' dat nigga shit!"

"Why are you punishing me for something that happened two years ago?" Karma asked in desperation.

"Because it shoulda neva happened!" Mekhi howled.

"But it did! And I've apologized to you for it time and time again, Mekhi!" Karma cried. "What else do you want me to do?"

"I want you to tell me if fuckin' my principal was worth killin' our relationship!"

Karma grimaced at the memory. Mekhi was supposed to be at swimming practice that early Saturday morning.

When he left for the day, Karma called Hassan and asked him to come over for breakfast. The two met initially in his office at Orange High School. Mekhi, a ninth grader at the time, had gotten into a fight with a classmate. Karma was called in, and she instantly caught Hassan's eye. She gave him her personal cell number for any matters concerning Mekhi, but he decided upon using it for personal reasons instead. One late night conversation led to another, and the two began to date.

That infamous morning began with Karma serving Hassan a plate of pancakes, eggs, grits, toast and orange juice. It concluded with Hassan showing his appreciation by bending her over the couch and violently thrusting in and out of her. Karma didn't hear the door open. She didn't see Mekhi enter the living room. She didn't even notice the swimming cap that he'd forgotten, lying in the accent chair. Karma let out one more moan of pleasurable pain before hearing, *"What the fuck?"* from the vestibule. She screamed Mekhi's name in horror as she and Hassan fell over themselves, trying to find fabric to cover their naked bodies.

"Ay, yo, what da fuck, man!" Mekhi screamed, charging at Hassan. "You fuckin' my mother?" He punched him in the face.

Hassan stammered backward, but quickly caught his steps. He lunged at the youngster, but Karma threw herself in between them. She pulled Mekhi away, who kept punching the air and screaming profanities and threats. He eventually shoved his mother off him.

"Get da fuck off me, trick!" he spat.

"What did you call me?" Karma asked, quickly losing her cool and slapping his face.

A brutal altercation ensued between them. Hassan, in his boxers, ran over to them and pried Karma's arm from around Mekhi's neck.

"You're no son of mine!" she screamed.

"I don't care! I don't care! I hate you!" he cried, sprinting out the door.

Karma shivered again at the nightmare that haunted her still. "No, it wasn't," she confessed. "But it also wasn't intentional."

"What about my father?" he asked unexpectedly.

"What about him?" Karma replied.

"Why didn't you tell me he was out?" Mekhi queried, placing his foot on the wall.

"Your sister tell you about his release?" Karma eyed him. Mekhi nodded.

Karma closed her eyes and ran her hand over her braid. "I was going to. I was just waiting for the right time." She sighed.

"I wanna meet him," Mekhi said, without warning.

"I can't allow that to happen."

"It's what Papa wanted, Ma. That's why I ran. I knew it was da end, and I didn't want to let 'im go. Before he lost consciousness, he told me to make peace wit' 'im. And dat's what I plan to do."

Karma, taken aback by her son's admission, covered her

mouth in an attempt to maintain her composure. This whole time she'd thought he ran out of fear. She'd labeled him a coward. But he wasn't. He was, instead, selfish. And she felt so guilty.

"If I allow you to—" Karma began slowly.

"Then I'll give Mr. Turner my blessing," he proclaimed. "We'll be even. I won't bring dat day up eva again. I'll put it behind me, apologize to him, and try to move forward . . . and be a betta son."

Karma took in everything Mekhi said. She looked in the distance, then refocused on him. "Your father loves you very much. He always has, but you are not ready to sit down with him. Not yet," she said, knowingly.

"I wanna know why he did it, Ma."

"We already told you, Mekhi," Karma replied with worried eyes.

"I know, but I wanna hear it from him."

"It will only hurt you." She took his face into her hands.

Mekhi slowly placed his hands over his mother's. "You're in here because of me. I'm da way I am because of him. Somethin's gotta give. Somethin's gotta change. *I've* gotta change. I see dat now." He sighed. "I wanna do right by you, Ma. I do. I fucked up . . . *bad.* You almost died," he said, choking back tears. "Give dis to me. Please?"

Karma stared into his sky blue eyes and smiled in defeat. "He's just going to hurt you again."

Chapter 17

"I don't know, man." Carmine shook his head. "This meeting that's supposed to happen between you and your pops. I don't know, bro. I mean, you're a better man than me. That's for sure. 'Cause I don't think I could sit down with the man who tried to kill me."

"It's what my grandfather wanted. And besides, if da nigga is still on some psychotic shit, it's gonna be da last time he eva sees me again," Mekhi confirmed. He shook his head and looked toward Springfield Avenue. Just as he turned back to face Carmine, Ekua walked out of the school with a group of girls. The two hadn't spoken since the night he was arrested. Mekhi tried to call and text her upon his release, even the days that followed, but she never responded. He even sent messages through his cousin and boys, yet she never called or texted him back. Unbeknownst to Mekhi, Ekua had made up her mind that he was a liability. And if they were meant to be together, their paths would cross again. One day.

Mekhi stepped away from Carmine and walked up to his estranged girlfriend. He looked down at her and waited for her to make eye contact with him. One of her girlfriends nudged her in the arm and nodded in Mekhi's direction.

Ekua followed her friend's eyes and exhaled quietly once she acknowledged his presence.

"Why haven't you returned any of my texts or calls?" Mekhi asked, angrily.

"You know why, Mekhi," Ekua replied in a hushed tone.

"No, I don't," he said, honestly. "That's why I'm askin'."

"Can we talk about this another time?"

"No. Right now is perfect," he grumbled. "Why you been avoidin' me, Ekua?"

"How's your mom?" Ekua replied in sincere concern.

"Don't worry 'bout how my mother is doin'. Dat's none of ya business," Mekhi snapped. "I'm askin' *you* why you been avoidin' me?"

"Because I didn't sign up for this, Mekhi." Ekua's eyes brimmed with tears. "You're too much for me. Your *rage* is too much for me. And if you don't get yourself together, you're going to get hurt or worse."

Mekhi raised his brow and pursed his lips. "What you really sayin' is when things get a little tough, you run."

"No, what I'm saying is I'm scared of you. You're dangerous, Mekhi, and you don't even know it."

"Dem niggas who came for me da otha night ain't gonna do it again, Ekua. Trust and believe dat," Mekhi replied with furrowed brows.

"Well, I don't, Mekhi. And you shouldn't either."

"It's not like I didn't tell you I have anger problems. I

told you about my past. All da shit I've been through."

"Yeah, but not to the extent that your friends did."

"My friends? What my friends got to do wit' you playin' me out?"

"Why don't you ask them. See you around." Ekua signaled to her friends that she was ready to go and they took heed.

"See you around?" Mekhi yelled to her back. "Dat's it? Dat's all I get?"

Ekua never looked back. She sauntered down the street until she and her friends disappeared around a corner.

Mekhi folded his hands on the back of his head and bit his bottom lip. "Yo, what da fuck?" he said, looking back at Carmine.

Carmine, uncomfortable, scratched the back of his neck and walked over to his best friend. "What happened? What she say?"

"She said some shit about you and Curt not believing dat da beef between me and dem South Ward niggas is squashed," Mekhi said, shifting his weight from one leg to the other. "Why would she say dat, C?"

Carmine tilted his head back and sighed heavily. "Me and Curt kinda told her to fall back from you when we were at da courthouse."

"What!" Mekhi snarled. "Yooo, what da fuck, man?"

"We're lookin' out for her, bro," Carmine explained. "You're caught up in some serious gang shit now, and we just don't want her to get hurt. We were doin' her a favor.

You and her, both. You would do da same if it were us."

"Nah, I wouldn't. I'd mind my muthafuckin' business and let you two niggas be happy."

"You're a target, bro," Carmine stressed. "You've got a bounty on your head. Put your feelings aside for a minute and look at it from our perspective. It's all da way fucked up!"

"Nah, what's fucked up is you and Curt cock blockin' a nigga." Mekhi seethed. "Y'all know how I feel about dat girl, and y'all ruined any chance of a future I had with her. Dat was some selfish shit, my dude."

"No, you're the selfish one, man," Carmine declared. "We didn't ruin anything. *You did.* You did *yourself* in, bro. The fight with those fools was one thing. You were defendin' yourself. She accepted that. But when you spat in 5-0's face and resisted arrest, dat's when shit got real for your girl. She saw all dat shit with her own eyes. And when I looked at her face, then I knew she wasn't sure if she was gonna stay wit' you or not."

"Y'all are haters, dude." Mekhi smiled crookedly. "I thought Jamie was da only one. But I see now, you and Curt ain't no different."

"How can you say dat shit to me?" Carmine fumed, meeting Mekhi face-to-face. "I've been your boy since the third grade. The third grade!"

Mekhi remained. Straight-faced.

"We were only tryin' to protect her. Somethin' you shoulda thought about doin'," Carmine jeered.

"We're through," Mekhi uttered, his top lip curled.

Carmine clenched his jaw against the pain. He loved Mekhi dearly and never thought their friendship would ever come to an end. "Fine," he snickered before turning and walking away.

Mekhi cursed into the wind before walking in the opposite direction. After walking less than half a block, he stopped suddenly and glanced around, checking to make sure he wasn't being watched. Seeing no one, Mekhi shook off the chill and gave a lengthy second glance. "I'm trippin'," he said as he strode forward with confidence. He couldn't, however, get rid of the chills running along his arms nor the warning in his gut. Had he just looked a little closer at the Honda civic parked on the corner, he would have seen the pair of eyes following him from behind its lightly tinted windows. It was there every day at the same, but Mekhi never took notice. Had he done so, he would have met Jamie's heavy, bloodshot eyes.

"*Maricon*." Jamie sat, blunt in hand, behind the wheel devising his next plan of attack.

Chapter 18

"Maybe this isn't a good idea after all," Karma said. "Everything might turn out all bad." She sat behind her office desk with her cell phone to her ear. She bounced back and forth in her leather high-back chair as she rested her index finger against her temple and tapped her foot against a cardboard box set at her feet.

"Baby, everything will be fine. Don't worry." Hassan was doing his best to calm her nerves on the other end as Money's arrival loomed over her.

Karma had been out of the hospital for two weeks and was grateful for her freedom. December had come with bitter winds and cloudy skies. Desiree's birthday was only a week away and she and Indigo had been running around from store to store like chickens with their heads cut off. Desi's special day was a big deal for the women in the family. It would be the last one spent at home with them.

Now, Karma ran down a list of things to do in her mind. She had to get Mekhi fitted for a tuxedo, Desi's shoes needed to be dyed; the list went on and on and on.

"How you feelin'?" Hassan asked.

"I don't know. I've been dreading this day for a long time." Karma exhaled.

"I know," Hassan said.

"I just want it to be over already." Karma tensed as her head throbbed. She rubbed her forehead in a measured pace.

"It will, baby. Just remember you're doing this for Mekhi."

"You're right. Enough about me. How about you? Are you sure you're okay with this?"

"I'm okay as long as you're okay." Hassan didn't want Money anywhere near Karma. He knew how hard she loved and lost him. And he didn't want Money to reignite a fire he put out two years ago.

"Of course, this is going to complicate things a little more, now that he's back in the picture," Hassan continued. "Damn, I really needed Mimi on my side on this." He sighed.

"You know what, babe? Let's just do it. Forget the kids," Karma said, waving her hand dismissively.

"What?" Hassan chortled in disbelief.

"Let's just go to City Hall and do it. Forget what I said before," Karma restated.

"You don't mean that, baby."

"Yes I do, honey. My kids are making major life decisions without me, whether I agree with them or not. I don't see why I can't do the same."

"Because it would be wrong. What they think and how they feel matters to you, babe. I know how important it is for you to have their blessing. So, I'll wait until things get straightened out with their father before I speak to them."

"Are you sure?"

A knock on the door sounded.

"I told you before, I'm not going anywhere," Hassan stated earnestly.

"Come in! Hold on, babe," Karma said into the phone as she looked toward the door.

Her uncle peeked his head in and smiled. "*Princessa*, there's a young lady out here who says she needs to speak with you. I cannot pronounce her name," Miguel uttered, his accent heavy.

"That's okay, *Tio*. Just send her in." Karma laughed.

"Okay." Miguel moved to the side, allowing Ekua to appear beside him in the doorway.

"Baby?" Karma said into the phone, smiling at the sight of Ekua.

"Yes, love?"

"I've gotta go. Mekhi's girlfriend just walked in." Karma smiled wider.

"Aiight, I'll call you later," Hassan replied. "Love you."

"Love you, too. Bye," she countered, ending the call with her thumb.

Karma placed the cellular device on her desk, then leaned back in her chair. She took in the teenage girl's gentle presence before folding her hands in her lap.

"Ekua." She nodded.

"Yes, ma'am," Ekua replied nervously.

"Come on in, honey, and have a seat."

"Okay." Ekua closed the door behind her. "Thank you." She smiled and sat across from her.

"You're very welcome. I've wanted to meet you for quite some time."

"Likewise, Ms. Walker." Ekua shifted in her seat. "I'm your number one fan. I've loved you since I was a little girl," she gushed. "I can't believe I'm talking to you right now."

"Well, believe it, baby." Karma blushed. "And thank you."

"You're welcome," Ekua said softly.

Karma rocked back and forth in her chair. "You've left quite an impression on my son."

"He's done the same." Ekua shifted again.

"I can imagine." Karma raised a brow. "A bad one, I gather."

"Not all bad." Ekua smiled.

She released a small sigh of relief. "Well, that's good to hear. So . . . to what do I deserve this honor?"

"I need to speak to you about Mekhi," Ekua replied, her pleasant face changing.

Karma placed her index finger on her cheek, bracing herself for what was to come. "All right. I'm listening."

Ekua studied her childhood shero's unruffled disposition before continuing. "I was with him, Desi, and his friends the night he got arrested. He didn't start the fight. Jamie, I think his name is, who he used to be friends with, had a gang member approach him on his behalf. That's how it all started."

"On his behalf?" Karma leaned forward slowly.

"Yes, ma'am." Ekua cleared her throat. "Because of what Mekhi did to his arm."

Again, Karma's head began to throb. She closed her eyes and placed her hand on her forehead, rubbing it slowly.

"Carmine and Curtis said they're all going to be after him now. On the day Mekhi was released, I told them they should tell you. But they said they'd take care of it." Ekua's voice quivered.

"Shit!" Karma hollered, banging her fist on the desk.

"I'm sorry, Ms. Walker."

"No, no, honey. Don't be sorry. You've done the right thing by telling me."

A loud silence befell.

"How is he?" Ekua asked cautiously.

"You don't know how he is?" Karma tilted her neck.

"No, ma'am. We're not together at the moment. I kinda broke it off because of everything that's going on."

"Well, that explains all the sulking he's doing around my house."

"Do you think I'm wrong for ending it?" Ekua's eyes glossed over.

"No," Karma replied firmly. "As a young woman, you're learning early that you have to do what's best for you in order to survive in this world. Even if it means hurting the ones you love or care about the most."

"He hates me now."

"He's hurt is all. Give him some time. Okay?"

"Okay. Thank you, Ms. Walker." Ekua rose from her chair.

Karma followed suit, relieved the girl didn't ask her to speak to Mekhi on her behalf, because she would have declined. She made it a point to never get involved with Mekhi's relationships.

"You're very welcome. Everything's going to be all right," she reassured her as they walked to the door. "Come on. Give me a hug." Karma allowed Ekua to fall into her outstretched arms. As they parted, Karma opened the door.

"Don't be a stranger now, you hear?"

"I won't." Ekua attempted a smile, and then made her way down the long, narrow hallway. "You remember your way back to the front entrance?"

"Yes, ma'am." Ekua turned back toward her.

"All right." Karma looked past the teenage ballerina and into the nearing eyes of her children's father.

Money smiled widely as he approached her. "Hey."

"Hey," Karma replied, returning a warm grin. "Come in . . . have a seat."

Money stepped in, closing the door behind him. He removed his wool skullcap from his head and took a seat in the chair opposite her desk.

In the sixteen years since they hadn't seen each other,

Karma couldn't help but notice how much muscle he'd packed on. Money's long beard was meticulously trimmed and well oiled. He still had those beautiful teeth and that smile; the infamous smile that reeled her in at her mother's birthday celebration. Karma couldn't deny it if she wanted to: Money was finer than he was when they first met. She shifted in her seat in discomfort.

"Thanks for coming." She grinned, her dimples peeking out.

"Of course," he replied. "I wouldn't miss this meeting for the world."

Karma blushed. She leaned back in her chair and folded her hands in her lap. "How are things going for you?"

"Good, good," Money replied truthfully. "I'm not living at the Y anymore."

"Really?" she asked in surprise.

"Yeah, I gotta little one-bedroom apartment on Lincoln Avenue in Orange," he expressed proudly.

"In Orange?" Karma replied with raised brows and wide eyes. She nearly lost her breath. She wouldn't dare tell him she lived only a few blocks away.

"Yeah, in the building closest to Heywood Ave.," Money replied.

"Oh . . . Okay," she said, hesitating. "I'm not familiar with the area," she lied. "But do you like it? Is it nice?"

"Oh, yeah. Yeah, it's cool," he admitted. "The street's quiet. The bus stop's right down the street. There's a papi store across the street from the bus stop. I get my spices

145

and snacks from there, you know? It's real convenient."

"That's good." Karma smiled. "I'm happy for you."

"Thank you." Money grinned. "Means a lot coming from you."

Karma blushed again. An awkward silence found its way into the room.

"Umm, before we start talkin' about Mekhi, I just want to take this time to thank you for sendin' my mom off the way you did. She looked beautiful," Money said.

Money, by law, was prohibited from attending his mother's funeral, so the correctional facility and funeral home made arrangements for him to pay his respects to her the day after her service. Two hours prior to her burial, Money was escorted by two corrections officers into The Family Funeral Home chapel. His hands and feet were cuffed; his head bowed in shame.

Evelyn lay at the front of the delicately lit room in a white and gold casket. She donned a white shroud with pearl earrings and matching necklace. Her makeup was light and her wig was styled in a curly bob. One of the CO's picked up a chair and set it near the head of the casket. Money shuffled toward his eternally still mother, then stopped a few feet away from her to allow the other CO to remove the handcuffs from his wrists. He trundled over to her and kneeled down on the stool at her casket. He placed his hand on hers and rested his other arm on the armrest attached to the stool. A wave of anguish overcame him as he set his eyes on her serene face. A low groan escaped from his lips, followed by a trail of tears. He hadn't known she was ill. She'd just suddenly stopped coming.

Money stayed at her side for an hour. He gave her a long kiss on the cheek before being handcuffed once again. A funeral director gave him a copy of the funeral program, two prayer cards, and allowed him to sign the guestbook before he left the funeral home for his trip back to the facility. Money remembered staring at all of the pictures of his mother and son in the booklet. Mekhi looked so much like him as a little boy. If there was any moment in his life where he was at his lowest, it was that day.

"You're welcome." Karma smiled small. "It was the least I could do. She did so much for me and the kids. It was only right."

The two shared a smile, locking eyes.

"Oh, before I forget," Karma said, retrieving the box from the floor and placing it on the desk. "I thought you might want your mom's things, so I boxed them up for you."

Money slid the box over in his direction. He pulled the flaps back and began to sort through the items. He found a photograph of Evelyn and the kids amidst the articles and pulled it out. He ran his thumbs over the picture, smiling sadly.

"Thank you," he said.

"Any time," Karma replied. "There should be a white envelope in there somewhere."

Curious, Money sifted through the box for the envelope. He found it.

"Your mother named you and the kids as her beneficiaries," Karma continued. "She had a life insurance policy for $450,000. Twenty thousand of it went to funeral costs. The other $430,000 was split down the middle between the three of you. She set up an account for you at Hudson City Bank. She frequented the branch on Main Street in Orange . . . in particular."

Money retrieved a miniature rectangular-shaped card out of the envelope. "Who's Junie Brown?"

"He's her financial advisor. Ask for him when you go see about your money."

"Okay." Money placed the business card and other documents back into the envelope.

"So," Karma countered. "Mekhi wants to meet you."

"Okay," he said carefully.

"But I have my reservations. He knows I do, but he doesn't care." She eyed him.

"May I ask why?" Money replied, folding his hands in his lap.

"He wants to know why you shot him, Money. And he's going to ask you. That's why."

"Are you afraid I'm goin' to rat you out?" Money asked seriously.

"I'm afraid of a lot of things. Not just that."

"I wouldn't do that to you, Karm. I love you too much to ever do somethin' like that to you."

Momentarily, Karma lost her breath

"I'm goin' to the grave with that," Money continued.

"If Mekhi wants to know why I did what I did, then I'm goin' to tell him. I'm man enough to admit I made a mistake. I made this mess. And I'm thankful that you've given me this opportunity to clean it up. So, that's what I'm goin' to do. I'm here to get my family back."

There were no signs of jesting on his face. Karma studied Money closely. He was dead serious.

Her cell phone vibrated atop the desk. "Sorry," she said softly.

"No need to apologize. Handle your business." He grinned.

Karma pulled her eyes away from the father of her children and set them on the blackened screen. She pressed the power button on the top of the electronic device and read the name on the screen. It read: INDIGO. She unlocked the gadget with the swipe of her thumb and read the message:

COME TO MY HOUSE AS SOON AS YOU GET OFF WORK!!!

Setting her phone back down, Karma stared at Money. He was seducing her with his eyes and her lady parts were responding to them.

"Can we talk more about this over dinner tomorrow night?" Money continued. "My treat."

"Oh, Money, I don't . . . I don't know." Karma shook her head from side-to-side.

"Please?" Money asked, his face serious. "It's just dinner."

Chapter 19

Karma placed an oven mitt on her hand as she walked over to the two ovens that were installed into the wall. She opened the bottom one, pulling out a tray of sizzling hot sirloin steaks before closing it once again. Mimi's two-week stay had come to an end. She was leaving in the morning. So she asked her mother, as she always did when she visited, to cook her one of her favorite dishes. Tonight it was steak, baked potatoes, salad, spinach, and Italian bread.

"*Mi amor*, can you set the table, please?" Karma asked while moving back toward the ovens and removing the pan of baked potatoes from the top one.

"Yes, ma'am," Mimi replied as she walked toward a set of mounted cabinets on the other side of the kitchen. "Smells good, Mommy."

"You hungry?" Karma chuckled.

"Am I?" Mimi smiled. "I'm so hungry, my stomach's touching my back." She laughed.

"Oh, my God!"

Mimi laughed at her mother's discomforted response.

"Well, everything's done. Hand me your plate," Karma

instructed.

"Mommy, you don't have to make my plate. I'm a big girl." Mimi smiled. "Go sit down. I'll make your plate instead."

"This is your night, baby," Karma reminded her. "Really, I don't mind."

"Ma," Mimi reiterated with a stern glance.

Karma raised her hands in submission. "All right, all right." She removed her apron and placed it on the island. She made her way into the dining room and sat down at the head of the table.

"What time is Mekhi getting in?" Mimi asked from the kitchen.

"He should be here in a little while," Karma replied, unfolding her cloth napkin and placing it in her lap. "The school van will drop him off."

"Okay." Mimi placed her mother's plate down before her.

"Thank you, baby." Karma smiled.

"You're welcome." Mimi settled down in the seat adjacent to hers. "Grace?"

"Will you, please?"

"Dear Lord, thank you for the food we're about to receive and the hands who prepared it. Thank you, Lord for sparing my mother's life. I pray that you continue to keep and cover her daily as well as my brother. Bring them peace so that they can live. Amen," Mimi concluded, raising her head. She and Karma's eyes met.

"That was beautiful, *mi amor*." Karma patted her wet eyes.

"Thanks, Mommy."

"So, when will you be back? In the spring?" Karma cut into her steak.

"Yeah. Most likely in May." Mimi buttered her potato. "Hopefully, in time for your birthday."

"That would be great. And I hope you'll bring Vivian with you also."

"I hope so, too, Mommy." Mimi blushed.

"You know your brother's going to be beside himself when you leave."

"He'll be all right."

"That's what I'm hoping for this time around. We had a long talk at the hospital."

"Yeah?" Mimi asked in surprise.

"Mm-hmm." Karma nodded.

"What did he say? Did he apologize for being a fuck up?"

Karma raised an eyebrow and pursed her lips. "Mimi," she said sternly.

"Sorry, Mommy. "Sorry. You were saying."

"We talked about my relationship with Hassan."

"Oh, yeah? How is your relationship with Mr. Tucker?" Mimi wiped her mouth with her napkin.

"It's good. Very good. He, uh, he asked me to marry him two weeks ago, but I told him I couldn't accept his proposal until I had you and your brother's blessing."

"Oh." Mimi sulked.

"What's the matter?" Karma asked in confusion. "I thought you liked him."

"I do like him. Very much."

"But."

"But now that Daddy's home . . ."

"Oh, honey, your father and I . . . that's a thing of the past."

"But he still loves you, Mommy."

"And how do you know that?"

"Because he told me so."

"When was this?"

"The day before Thanksgiving. I went to his job and spoke to him," Mimi admitted hesitantly. "Told him what was going on between you and Mekhi."

"I beg your pardon?" Karma's brows furrowed. She slowly placed her fork down on the plate, then rested her forearms on the edge of the table.

"I said—"

"I heard what you said. I'm just trying to understand why you would divulge that information to him, Mimi?"

"Because he's our father, Mommy, and I really think he can do something about Mekhi's temper."

"Just like he did the last time?" Karma snatched her napkin off her lap and flung it onto the table. She picked up her plate and eating utensils, then traveled into the kitchen.

She set her dishes onto the island as Mimi rose from her chair and entered the kitchen thereafter.

"Mommy," Mimi pleaded.

"You were too young to understand what was going on at the time." Karma shook her head at the memory. "And trust me, it hurt to turn him in, but seeing that hole he put in your brother's back hurt so much more. Your father was dangerous then and he's dangerous now, Mimi."

"I think you're wrong, Mommy. I don't think he'll hurt Mekhi again. I don't think he'll hurt any of us."

"You don't know what he's going to do. Mental illness is incurable, honey. It doesn't just go away with medicine and treatments," Karma countered. "All that stuff just keeps it under control . . . in hibernation. Your father is a sick man, and he always will be."

"Let me be the judge of dat," Mekhi said, walking into the dimly lit space. "Let me decide whether I wanna deal wit' 'im or not, after everything is said and done."

Karma looked back and forth between her son and daughter. Both of them were spitting images of Money and steadfast in their convictions.

"I wish you both could see what I see when I look into his eyes." Karma sighed.

"There's going to come a day when you'll have to stop protecting us, Mommy. Not just from Daddy," Mimi uttered.

"See, that's where you're wrong, *mija*. Because that'll never happen. Not as long as I'm a mother—*your* mother—

and I have breath in my body." Karma hurried past her children and out of the room. "I'm going to Indigo's." She snatched her coat, keys and pocketbook off of the island, then made her way out the door. Slamming it shut.

"She's having sex. I know it." Indigo sulked, gripping a pair of blood-stained panties in her hand. She paced back and forth in her daughter's room.

Karma sat at the foot of Desi's bed, watching her cousin tread the carpeted floor. "You don't know that for sure, *prima*," she replied calmly.

"Oh, no? Then why else would she hide these at the bottom of her hamper?" Indigo queried.

"She could have had an accident. And why are you going through her things?" Karma asked in astonishment.

"No, no. Mommy found them when she was about to do the laundry," Indigo explained.

"Well, did either of you find any other soiled pairs?" Karma quizzed.

"No," Indigo replied, stopping in her tracks.

Despondently, Karma sighed. She felt awful for her cousin. Indigo was such a good mother. She always went out of her way to give Desiree whatever she needed. That girl wanted for nothing. Indigo and Stuff both, made sure of it.

"I don't know what to say, *prima*," Karma expressed.

"She's only seventeen-years-old! *Seventeen!*" Indigo

screamed, her eyes filling with tears. "My God. Does she know she can never get that back?" She wept.

Karma rose from the bed and took her sister-cousin into her arms and held her with all of her might. She refused to let her fall. She and Indigo had been through hell and back. This was the first time, in a long time, that Karma was at a loss for words. No mother wanted their daughter to give away something so precious at such a young age. An age where she was still growing and learning. Unlike Indigo, Karma was well aware of Mekhi's promiscuity. Even though she didn't approve of it, she accepted it and supplied him with condoms. She stayed on that boy, making sure he used the contraception and got tested every six months.

The begging question now was if Desi really was sexually active. And if so, was the girl using protection. Karma hoped she was taking the necessary precautions to protect herself. Because if she wasn't, God only knew what kind of wrath Indigo was going to bring down on that child. And that was a fury no one had ever seen.

Chapter 20

She still had Desi's panties in her clutches. Indigo sat on the edge of her bed, legs agape, and her head hung. Maggie stood at the window, looking out while Karma stood beside her cousin, rubbing her back. It was after nine o'clock. Desi was nowhere to be found. Karma decided to stay with Indigo after her breakdown. She didn't trust her. Her cousin was in a fragile state. She'd stopped talking hours ago. Not a good sign. So, Karma thought it best to stick around just in case a fight broke out between mother and daughter.

The opening and closing of the front door sounded. All three women looked toward the entryway, waiting for Desi to trail the stairs. The pitter-patter of her feet ascending the stairwell filled the hallway. It then came to an abrupt halt. Karma could see her niece's shadow come into view along the wall in the hallway. Desi's figure soon appeared in her mother's doorway. She made eye contact with each of them before waving and giving them a nervous smile.

"Hey . . . everybody."

"Do you know what time it is?" Maggie asked with her hands on her hip.

"I know, Nana. I'm sorry—" Desi began.

"De fright you gave your mother?" Maggie interrupted her.

"I was hanging out with my friends and lost track of time," she said with a straight face.

Indigo raised a brow and shook her head. "Do you think we're stupid?

"No," Desi replied.

"Then why are you standing there lying?" Indigo asked, with a disgusted smirk.

"I'm not—"

"Stop." Indigo raised her hand. "Just stop." She unrolled the underwear and held them up by her index finger.

"Your grandmother found these in the bottom of your hamper. Are you using protection?"

Desiree gulped hard. "Mommy—"

"Answer your mother, gal," Maggie ordered.

Desiree cast her eyes toward her feet. The jig was up. "Sometimes," she murmured.

"I God!" Maggie said, slapping her thighs.

Karma looked away as Indigo stared coldly into the glassy emerald green eyes of the child whom she brought into the world.

"I love him," Desi mumbled.

Indigo, unexpectedly hauled off and slapped her hard across the face. Desi stumbled backward, and then fell onto the floor. Without warning, her mother pounced on her, straddling her and throwing wild punches. Karma and Maggie ran over to them and struggled to pull Indigo off the shaken teen.

"Mommy, please! Please, stop hitting me!" Desi balled. "I'm pregnant!"

"What?" Indigo screamed, staring down at the flush-faced girl. She blacked out completely and grabbed a handful of Desi's hair with her left hand and punched her mercilessly in the face with her right. Blood flew all over the place. Maggie and Karma tried their hardest to break them apart, but their strength was no match for Indigo's.

"What the hell?" Stuff hollered, running into the room. He immediately pried his wife off their daughter, kicking and screaming obscenities.

Karma kneeled beside her fallen niece, taking her bloody face into her hands. Desi had a large, deep gash across her forehead. Her nose was bleeding and her left eye was swelling shut.

"We need to call an ambulance!" Karma urged.

"Me call," Maggie replied, leaving Stuff and Indigo's side. She trotted out of the room.

"And a towel, *Tia!*"

"What the hell is going on in here?" Stuff shouted as Indigo snatched her arm out of his grasp.

"She's pregnant!" She wept hysterically.

"What? By who? Not dat nigga?" he growled, looking back and forth between Indigo and Karma. "Oh, nah. Nah, nah, nah!" he snarled, punching a hole in the wall nearest to him.

"I'm sorry, Daddy," Desi whimpered, aimlessly kicking her legs beneath her.

Maggie jogged back into the room and handed Karma a towel. Karma applied the towel to her niece's head as her aunt bent down on the other side of Desi, taking her bloody hand into hers.

"Shhh, it's all right. Everyting's going to be all right," Maggie comforted her.

"I'ma kill 'im!" Stuff barked, storming toward the door.

"Daddy, no! Nooo!" Desi sobbed, reaching for her father's foot.

Stuff shook his foot out of his daughter's grasp and sprinted down the stairwell and out the door.

Chapter 21

HIGH SCHOOL BASKETBALL STAR FOUND IN PARK

By Amal Melton/The Star-Ledger
December 3, 2017

The body of a dark-skinned male found in a field in the Belleville section of Branch Brook Park has been identified as high school basketball star, Curtis Johnson III, 15, of South Orange. A jogger made the gruesome discovery yesterday morning just off Mill Street, not far from the spot where Wesley Stewart's body was found last month.

The county prosecutor's office said Johnson, who was beaten, castrated, and bound by his hands and feet, may have died somewhere else, and later been left in the park. He was reported missing by family last evening. He was last seen by friends and family two days ago at a routine basketball practice in the gymnasium of Newark's St. Benedict's Prep where Johnson was a sophomore. He was dubbed "the next Magic Johnson," and was ranked number one in the nation and named the best high school basketball player in the country earlier this year. He recorded a triple double of, 36 points, 18 rebounds and 16 assists in his last game against Paterson's East Side High.

The Medical Examiner has not determined the cause or manner of death. Autopsy results by the Regional Medical Examiner's Office are still pending.

Karma pulled into Indigo's driveway, shutting her car off thereafter. Seeing the newspaper article about Curtis's murder had thrown her for a loop.

She turned the sunvisor down and retrieved the key to the house. She climbed out of her car, closed the door with her hip, then walked up the brick-layered walkway to the back entrance. As she placed the key into the keyhole, Karma took a deep breath in, then exhaled in an attempt to maintain her composure. She wanted to be as calm and collected as possible. Karma turned the key and the doorknob in syncopation as she gently pushed the heavy wooden structure open.

"Knock, knock," she said softly as she spotted Indigo moving between the island and the stove.

"Hey," Indigo replied, never meeting her eyes. "Have you had breakfast yet?"

"No," Karma answered as she closed the door.

"All right. Well, fried potatoes, cheese grits, and omelettes with ham and spinach in them are on this morning's menu, if you're hungry," Indigo said, keeping busy.

She moved about the room without missing a beat. Karma knew Indigo was obviously bothered by Curtis's murder also. Her shiftiness said it all.

"Have you read this morning's paper?" She eyed her closely.

Indigo picked up a spatula and flipped one of the omelettes. "No, I haven't," she replied, still avoiding eye contact.

"No?" Karma asked in surprise.

"No." Indigo shook her head nonchalantly, placing the cooked omelette on a plate. Then adding a scoop of fried potatoes and cheese grits to it.

"Has Stuff?" Karma continued as Indigo placed the plate of hot food before her. "Thank you."

"I don't know." Indigo shrugged, retrieving a fork and napkin out of one of the island's drawers. She set the items beside Karma's plate, thereafter. "Want some juice?"

"No, thank you," Karma said, slightly reclining in the stool. Watching her still.

"Okay." Indigo rubbed the beads of sweat forming on her forehead with the back of her hand.

"Stuff gets the paper every Sunday. Are you telling me he hasn't seen the article about Curtis yet?" Karma cocked her head to one side.

"No, I'm telling you I don't know if he's gotten the paper yet. And if he has, he hasn't said anything to me about—that," Indigo stated, matter-of-factly, finally meeting Karma's gaze.

"You need to be ashamed of yourself right now. Lying to me the way you are." Karma shook her head. "Why didn't you tell me Stuff really went after that boy?"

"Because he told me he didn't," Indigo huffed. "And I believe him."

"The man stormed out of here last week ranting and raving about how he was going to kill that boy, and today, the child is in the paper. *Dead.* That isn't a goddamn coincidence, Indigo!" Karma pushed her plate of food aside.

"He said he didn't do it, Karma," Indigo said sternly. "And I believe him."

Leaning back a little in her stool, Karma stared at her cousin in disbelief. Either Indigo was in denial, or Desi's pregnancy had really done a number on her mentally. Whether Karma knew it or not, it was a little bit of both. Indigo had poured all of her hopes and dreams into her daughter. The girl had a promising future, and she'd ruined it overnight. Then her husband, who she'd thought left his criminal past in that place and time, reverted back to the cold-blooded killer she fell in love with as a teenage girl. Indigo's life was falling apart right before her eyes, and she didn't know how to put the pieces back together.

Karma's brows slowly knitted together as she watched Indigo turn away from her and rest her hands on the edge of the sink. She stared out the window, setting her eyes on anything in her sightline.

"Does Desi know?"

"Mm-hmm." Indigo nodded before dropping her head and breaking down into tears.

"Oh, *prima*," Karma countered, just above the whisper. She rose from her seat and moved toward her. Karma wrapped her arms around her, enveloping her tightly. Indigo allowed her head to fall back onto Karma's shoulder. She grabbed hold of her hands and continued to let her tears fall.

"Everything is going to be all right," Karma whispered in her ear as the two began to rock side-to-side.

"She won't come out of her room." She hiccupped.

"Do you want me to go up and try to talk to her?" Karma asked gently.

Indigo simply shook her head.

"Okay, okay." Karma squeezed tighter.

The sound of slipper-covered feet caught Karma's attention. She continued to whisper words of encouragement in Indigo's ear as her aunt Maggie entered the kitchen with an empty coffee mug and saucer in hand. The two made eye contact immediately.

"I God." Maggie sucked her teeth as she hurriedly placed the mug and saucer down on the island. She shuffled over to her niece and daughter, placing her hands on both of them. "Me got her, baby," Maggie assured Karma.

"Okay." Karma nodded with worry. "And Stuff?" she asked, moving out of her aunt's way.

"In the office," the elder replied, wiping Indigo's tears with the palm of her hands.

"Thank you, Tia." Karma barely smiled before marching out of the room and toward Stuff's office.

She walked to the other side of the room, settling before a beautifully carved cherry wood door. She knocked on it hard. Three times.

"Come in," his deep, gritty voice commanded behind the heavy structure.

Turning the knob, Karma stepped onto a deep red carpet that stretched from one end of the room to the other. Outlining the base of the multiple framed certificate-covered walls.

"Hey, sis," he cooed, with the day's paper hanging in mid-air. His face concealed by it. "I knew it was you."

"How's that?" Karma sat down across from him.

"Because you're da only one who knocks on a door like da muthafuckin' pigs." Stuff chuckled.

"I don't know how you can laugh at a time like this. I really don't," Karma frowned. "Your wife is in the kitchen crying her eyes out. She's lying to me as well as herself about what happened to that boy. And your daughter . . . from what I was told, is upstairs in her room and won't come out. How the hell can you laugh about *anything* right now?"

Stuff folded the paper together, then placed it down on his desktop. He ran his hand across his mouth as he leaned back in his leather high-back chair and stared into Karma's honey-brown eyes.

"How could you, Stuff?" Karma leaned forward. "You couldn't have just scared him?"

"I swear on our parents, I didn't kill dat nigga," Stuff replied.

"Then what about sanctioning it?" Karma replied,

knowing better.

He sighed before averting his eyes. Stuff could never get over on Karma. She or her late mother. He'd been responsible for too many murders and disappearances over the years. And even though neither women had proof of Stuff's involvement, his active status in the drug game was enough validity for them.

"That's what I thought," Karma spat, reclining. "Did you ever once think about how our kids were going to be affected by this shit? Huh?"

Stuff shook his head.

"Mekhi's without a friend, Stuff. A very good friend. And your grandchild is without a father," Karma ranted.

"Hold up." Stuff waved his hand.

"Hold up, nothin'!" Karma countered. "Whether you want to accept it or not, Desiree is pregnant, and Curtis was the father of that baby. You could have taken a better course of action, but you were so caught up in whatever dreams you and Indigo had for that girl, you snatched those same dreams from his parents."

Stuff's jaw clenched and unclenched as he listened to his best friend closely. There was no point of arguing, because she was right. He'd gone off the deep end, upon learning of Desi's pregnancy.

"Desi . . . is never going to look at you the same again, Stuff. She's going to hate you. And she's going to hate you for a long time. I hope you're prepared for it, my brotha, because it hurts. It hurts like hell," Karma confessed. She rose from her seat and walked out of the room, leaving Stuff still and in deep thought.

Chapter 22

He couldn't believe his boy was gone. Mekhi lay sprawled out in his bed with his hands folded behind his head. The newspaper article lay beside him. He stared up at the ceiling, reminiscing about the endless days and nights he spent with Curtis. He couldn't believe he'd knocked up his cousin. Of all the girls to impregnate, it had to be Desi. Mekhi knew he shouldn't have given Curtis permission to pursue her. But he figured his friend would chase after her whether he wanted him to or not. He had no idea who'd gotten a hold of him and killed him. The crew had so many enemies, it could have been anyone.

"Damn, man," Mekhi said as a tear rolled down the side of his eye.

A knock on his bedroom door sounded.

"Mekhi?" Karma called softly.

"Yeah?" he replied in a low, cheerless tone.

"May I come in?" she asked.

"Yeah," he responded, wiping his eyes.

Karma slowly opened the door and grimaced at the sight of her depressed man-child. She walked over to the bed and sat at the foot of it. She placed her hand on his legs and rubbed them lovingly.

"How are you holding up?" she asked gently.

"Aiight, I guess." Mekhi shrugged. "I don't know. I mean, what happened to Curt is da type of stuff you hear on da news all da time. I just neva thought it would happen to any of us. At least, I always hoped it wouldn't."

"I know, baby," Karma cooed.

"He didn't deserve it, man," Mekhi whispered, covering his tear-filled eyes with his fists. "He didn't deserve it."

Karma scooted toward Mekhi's torso, placing one hand on his rib and the other over his heart. She watched her son weep like the baby he was so long ago. Helpless. There was nothing she could say or do to take his pain away. It was the same pain she embodied when her mother was taken. It was without warning, without repentance. Mekhi would have to embrace it like she had, then accept the disconcerting stillness that lasted for countless nights thereafter.

"It's going to be okay, baby." She sniffled. "It is. It's going to hurt for a while, but the pain will ease with time."

"He was da only one who supported my decision to go to da Army after graduation." Mekhi shook his head.

Karma took a deep breath in, then released it. She was still against Mekhi signing his life away to the military. Even though he hadn't gotten to a recruiting office yet to do so, she knew he would once time allowed.

"He was a very good friend. A real sweetheart." She sighed, biting her tongue. "We're all going to miss him."

"How's Desi?" Mekhi asked, wiping his eyes.

"Not good," Karma replied. "Maybe you can give her a call, if or when you feel up to it."

"Yeah." Mekhi nodded. "Aiight." He inhaled, then released a heavy breath.

"Listen. I need to ask you something," Karma began, her face serious.

"Okay," Mekhi replied quietly.

"The night you were arrested . . . when you told me you were jumped by a gang from Newark and you didn't know who they were . . . was that the truth?" Karma eyed him.

Mekhi averted his eyes, then looked back at his mother. She waited patiently. "No."

Karma sighed heavily.

"It was Jamie and his crew."

"Mekhi." She rubbed her forehead. "Why didn't you tell me?" Karma struggled to understand.

"Because I didn't want you worryin' for no reason," Mekhi confessed. "I still don't."

"Oh, no, but there *is* a reason, *mi vida*. And I'm looking at him right now."

"He ain't gonna do nothin', Ma. He's a punk."

"Which is more reason for him *to* do something, honey. Come on, you know better. Your grandfather and I. . .your uncles, we all taught you the game. Punks don't fight fair. Punks don't fight at all. Not these days. No. Now, they just shoot."

"Ma. Me and C are gonna take care of it," Mekhi huffed.

"No, what you are going to do is allow *me* to take care of it. I don't want you leaving this house unless it's for school or practice. Is that understood?"

"Ma." Mekhi sulked.

"I'm not going to lose you over bullshit, Mekhi. In fact, I'm going to go up to the school on Monday and speak to Father Doherty about this."

Mekhi shook his head. This was the exact reason he didn't tell her the truth.

"Carmine is more than welcome to come over here and hang or whatever. But, *you*—you are on house arrest until I say otherwise. *Comprende?*"

"Yeah," Mekhi replied hesitantly.

"Good." Karma brushed his cheek with her hand.

Mekhi closed his eyes under her touch, then reopened them. He stared at her for a moment; her face was lightly made up and she was dressed in a beautiful paisley print Indian tunic in peacock hues, leggings, and Nine West "'Pearson"' knee-high heeled boots. Her hair was pulled back into a large chignon and her bronzed skin dabbed with Chanel No. 5 perfume.

"You goin' somewhere?" he quizzed.

"Yes." She nodded.

"Where?" Mekhi pried more.

"To dinner," she replied evenly. "With your father."

Mekhi's eyebrows rose in wonderment.

"No, not like that. I'm just meeting him at Don Pepe's to talk about you—and this meeting that you both want so badly."

"Oh. Well, you look good."

"Do I?" Karma blushed, taken aback by Mekhi's admittance.

"Yeah, you do. Real pretty, Ma."

"Thank you, beloved." She smiled, stroking his cheek.

"Does Mr. Turner know you and—" Mekhi inquired openly.

"Yes, he does," Karma lied. "There are no secrets between him and me. It's called communication." She grinned.

As awful as she felt for lying to Mekhi, Karma knew Hassan would not approve of the dinner between her and Money. Dinners were intimate. Dinners at fancy restaurants were even more intimate. She didn't want Hassan to think more of the dinner than it really was. Besides, many a business deal happened over dinner.

"Oh. He texted me a little while ago."

"He did?"

"Yeah. You put 'im up to it, didn't you?"

"No." She shook her head fervently. "I had absolutely nothing to do with him reaching out to you."

"Oh."

"If you don't mind me asking. What did he say?" Karma shifted her weight.

"He just told me to keep my head up. And if I need anything, to talk or whateva . . . he's here for me." He sniffled.

"And he means it, baby." Tears filled her eyes again. "All right. Well, let me get going. I know you don't have much of an appetite, but I made dinner anyway. I put your plate in the oven."

"Aiight. Thank you."

"You're welcome. I won't be gone long." She rose from the bed. "Call me if you need me."

"Nah. I'm tryin' to break dat habit," Mekhi teased.

With his hands folded beneath his chin, Money watched Karma sip her glass of white Sangria. He'd missed her full, inviting lips. Never in a million years did he ever think he was going to get the opportunity to break bread with her again. The young woman whom he'd fallen in love with sixteen years ago, now sat before him as a full-grown, *mature* woman. She'd been to hell and back more times than she could count. But she always returned stronger than the last . . . each and every time.

Karma met Money's gaze as she gently placed her glass down on the table. She thought the Sunni beard he was sporting was very becoming. It was well-trimmed and oiled. It made him look distinguished.

"You're staring again." She blushed.

"I can't help it. You're beautiful," Money admitted with a slight tilt of his head. "You're as beautiful now as you were when I first saw you at your mother's birthday party."

Slowly, Karma turned her face. The last thing she wanted to be reminded of was that God-awful night. She could feel the tears creeping up from the back of her eyes. So she closed them and tried to refocus on the purpose for this dinner.

"I'm sorry," Money said softly. "I didn't know it still upset you."

"Of course it still upsets me, Money," Karma spat, cutting her eyes at him. "You were there. You saw what he did to her."

"You're right. I did." He nodded. "I apologize. I don't know what I was thinking."

Money shifted in his seat, then cleared his throat in discomfort. The dinner wasn't going the way he wanted. He had to think of something meaningful to say and quickly.

"You know, I waited sixteen years for this moment," he began. "I prayed for it. Prison . . . is a horrible place to be. A man has to keep his mind on something or *someone* to get him through. And that was you, Karm. Thoughts of you. The memories of all the good times we shared. That's what kept me going . . . kept me sane."

Karma looked back at Money in search of the monster she knew lived inside of him. But she found nothing but warmth behind his gaze.

"And what about the kids? Did you ever think about them?"

"No," Money replied earnestly.

"No?" Karma asked in confusion.

"No. Because the one time I did, I almost lost my life," he professed. "Kids and mothers remind you of how greatly you fucked up on the outside. The thought of their existence makes a man weak . . . vulnerable. They're a liability in there."

"Oh." Karma gulped.

"So, that left you . . . and it *began* . . . with you also." Money grinned kindly, his eyes intense and steady.

Although Karma could feel the heat rising in her body, she didn't understand what was happening. Karma didn't know why she was becoming flushed under this man's glare. His words were genuine, but his stare was that of hunger and regret. She didn't know why he still had this effect on her. After all he had done to her and their son. He didn't deserve this reaction. *Hassan* didn't deserve it either.

"Excuse me . . . for a moment," she managed to say as she rose from her seat.

"Everything all right?" Money queried, rising also.

"Mm-hmm." Karma nodded, sashaying away.

She pushed through the heavy wooden doors to the women's restroom with all her might. Karma placed her clutch down on the sink and stared back at her reflection in the mirror. Her cheeks were pink, her lips swollen. She shook her head in disbelief and sighed. This dinner was supposed to be a discussion about their son. *How did he make it about her?* Karma turned the faucet on and cupped her hands beneath the rushing water. She didn't care if her make-up was going to be completely washed away. She needed to cool down. Karma splashed her face with cold water, patting her hot cheeks with her fingertips. The opening of the bathroom door sounded. Then the clicking of its lock. Karma, oblivious to the presence moving toward her back, continued to dab/douse her face. She ran her fingers over her closed eyes before shutting the faucet off and reopening them. Money stood behind her, staring back at their reflection. He moved forward, filling the space between them. He pressed his hardened manhood against her back and watched her chest rise and fall. Wrapping his left arm around her muscled waist, he slid his right hand between her breasts before massaging them. Money leaned into her neck and kissed it tenderly. Then he licked the nape of her neck, kissing the other side the same. Karma closed her eyes and grabbed Money's hands with her own. Money ran their clutched hands from her full breasts, past her firm stomach, to her aching lips between her legs. He gently broke free from her tight grasp, bringing his hand to his mouth. He licked his fingers and forced them between Karma's skin and the fabric of her leggings clinging to it once again. He slid past her pulsating lips and into her wet, tight channel. Karma threw her head back and grabbed hold of Money's button-down shirt collar. She was losing herself and didn't know how to regain control.

"I missed you, baby," Money panted in her ear.

"Mmm," Karma moaned.

"I need you, Karma," Money groaned. "I need to be

inside of you."

Her knees buckled. She was light-headed. What they were doing wasn't right. She had a good man. Hassan was a good man, and he deserved better.

"No," Karma whimpered.

"Please," Money begged, sucking on her neck.

"No, Money," Karma repeated, reaching for his hand. "No. This . . . doesn't belong . . . to you . . . anymore."

Money opened his eyes, his hand slowly creeping out of Karma's pants.

"What?"

"I'm involved—with someone." Karma peered back at him, removing his hand completely from her panties and his arm from around her waist.

A smile of disbelief appeared on Money's face. He stepped back, then ran his hand over his beard. The thought of Karma moving on never crossed his mind. Not while he was in prison or on the outside. He'd somehow convinced himself that she would keep the most precious part of herself to *herself.* Then give it back to him when she thought he was deserving.

"Who?" He winced in dismay.

"I have to go." Karma sighed regrettably.

"Who, Karma?" Money asked again, his pain evident.

"You don't know him. Listen, I'll call you when Mekhi's ready. He just lost one of his best friends, so I don't know how long that's going to be."

"Karma."

"Money. Damnit!" Karma stamped her foot and snatched her purse from the sink. She unlocked the restroom door, then hurried out.

Chapter 23

Mekhi stood at Curtis' grave with his hands buried deep in the pockets of his black label coat. Even with the black and silver metal casket lying before him, he couldn't believe his dear friend was gone. First his grandfather, now Curtis. Mekhi didn't know how many more losses he could take. As far as he was concerned, this wasn't living. He was merely existing.

He bit the inside of his cheek as his eyes pulled him to a figure standing behind a row of headstones at the top of one of the cemetery's many hills. Jamie, his head covered with a yellow and black baseball cap and matching North Face thermoball vest, looked down at Mekhi with pursed lips. A conversation began between the two former friends; unspoken. Unsettled business confirmed. Mekhi tilted his head back and clenched his jaw as a challenge to the liberated gangbanger. Jamie simply smiled in response.

"He ain't even worth lookin' at, bro," a familiar voice spoke from behind Mekhi. Mekhi smirked and nodded.

Carmine settled beside his estranged best friend, setting his eyes on the casket before them. The two hadn't spoken since the day of their argument. Of course they still shared a number of classes together as well as swim practices and meets, but they never talked. Not until now.

"Dis shit, right here . . . is fucked up, bruh," Mekhi finally said.

"Yeah, it is." Carmine sniffled.

"We all were supposed to—we all were supposed to make it *together*," Mekhi went on. "And now it's ova. It's all ova." He looked over at Carmine, then back at Curtis' casket.

". . . How's Desi?" Carmine asked.

Mekhi sighed at the thought of his heart-broken cousin. "Desi. Desi ain't talkin'. She ain't eatin', she ain't talkin' . . . she ain't sleepin'. She ain't doin' much of anything."

"We gotta be strong for her, bro. For each other." Carmine eyed him. "It's just us now. I know what she and Curt had was young and new, but he really loved her. He told me so."

"Word?" Mekhi asked.

"Word. And he was happy about the baby. He was gonna do right by them. Marry Desi and all." Carmine choked back tears.

A tear rolled down Mekhi's cheek. He was happy to know Curtis held his cousin in the highest regard. It was much more than he could say for himself.

"You know . . . you and Curt were right." He nodded. "I shoulda had Ekua's best interest at heart. I fucked up, all the way around."

"She'll forgive you, like I have," Carmine assured him. "As soon as you put yourself aside, get outta ya own way . .

. she'll come back. And then she'll stay."

"You think so?" Mekhi asked, looking back over at him again.

"Yeah, man. I do." Carmine smiled. "You're my brotha. I wouldn't lie to you."

"No, you wouldn't," Mekhi said just above a whisper. "Because what hurts my brotha—"

"Hurts me," Carmine concluded.

The two embraced in a strong, heartfelt hug before staring up at the top of the hill again. Jamie was gone. How symbolic. Everyone and everything the boys had once known and loved was—gone.

Karma watched the exchange between the two young men from behind the wheel of her car. She'd seen Jamie appear at the hilltop and waited for him to make a move, any move toward Mekhi. She was uncertain if he'd come to the cemetery alone or with his crew. Either way, she was ready for whatever pain Jamie thought he was going to bring.

She looked down at her watch. The two o'clock hour was approaching. She had to get back to the Montclair location soon. Although it was in good hands, that of her uncle's, she didn't like putting more work on him than necessary. Her mind wandered to the other night, the dinner with Money. He'd left her a slew of messages on her answering machine at the Newark location. Some were filled with rage, others with sadness. All ended with a request to see her again, but she had yet to return any of his calls. There was nothing left to say about their sexual encounter. It shouldn't have happened, and Karma was going to make sure there would be no repeats.

Someone knocking on her driver-side window broke Karma out of her reverie. She looked through its tint and smirked at the sight of the young man who wanted her son dead. Karma rolled the window down.

"Jamie." She smiled.

"Hey, Ms. Walker." Jamie smiled also.

"How are you? I didn't see you at the service."

"I sat in da back."

"Oh, okay. Look, why don't you get in? Sit with me for a little while and catch up. I haven't seen you in months."

Jamie, caught off guard, hesitated for a moment. He briefly looked at his former friends in the distance, then made his way to the passenger side of the luxury vehicle. He settled into the warmth of its heated leather seats.

"What's good, Ms. Walker?" Jamie blinked at her innocently.

"You tell me," Karma replied lightly. "How are you?"

"I'm straight." He shrugged. "Can't really complain."

"Good. That's good to hear. And your mom. How is she?"

"Oh, she's doin' real good." Jamie smiled proudly. "She just made assistant manager at the Walmart in Kearny."

"That's wonderful!" Karma grinned. "She's a hard

worker, your mom. *Diligent*. And we don't want her to have to work any harder than she already does, do we?"

"I don't know wha'chu mean," Jamie admitted, his brows pinched together.

"I mean, to pay for your funeral," Karma said with the raise of her brow.

Jamie watched the older woman's eyes turn dark, as if the sun was setting in them. He shifted in his seat.

"Because I can make that happen," Karma continued. "I know you're after Mekhi for breaking your arm. It shouldn't have happened, and I truly am sorry for what he did to you. I paid all your medical bills and even went as far as paying for your therapy. That was the right thing to do. But you are the one who decided not to go. So, here we are. This isn't the way to go about things, *chico*. And if you don't stop, I'm going to be forced to *make you stop*."

"He ended my fuckin' career!" Jamie shouted.

"And I will end your fuckin' life! If anything . . . and I mean *anything*, happens to my son, I'm going to kill you. Then I'm going to show up at your funeral and give your mother my condolences personally," Karma said, without batting an eye.

"Ay, yo, Ms. Walker . . ." Jamie repeated.

"Ay, yo, what?" Karma said. "What?"

"Yo, you talkin' real greasy right now."

"Touch my son and see how much more greasy I can get," Karma spat. "You'll be nothing more than a muthafuckin' memory after I get through with you. A photograph on a T-shirt."

Jamie's eyes shrank into a squint. He gave her a once-over before opening the door and exiting the car. Karma never took her eyes off him. She watched him rub his nose nervously as he trekked down the long, winding cemented path, disappearing behind snow-covered trees and aged monuments.

Chapter 24

"I don't know, baby. You're getting in pretty late tonight. Are you sure you're still going to want to go out and eat? You're certain?" Karma asked Hassan through her Bluetooth.

"Absolutely," Hassan replied sternly. "We'll have dinner, then go home and bless that new hot tub you got in the backyard."

"What? You have lost your mind. It's going to be eighteen degrees tonight."

"You won't feel it. Trust me." Hassan chuckled.

Karma blushed. She liked the sound of that. Still, she felt guilty for what transpired between her and Money a week ago. Tonight, she was going to make sure Hassan never questioned his place in her life.

"Okay." Karma giggled. "I'll see you later."

"Later, babe," Hassan cooed.

Karma pulled into the Loews movie theatre parking lot in Wayne and parked between a moving truck and a Nissan with a boot on its front left tire. She turned the engine off and studied the back of her son's head. Mekhi looked out the window, taking in the abstract-constructed building. He was moments away from meeting the man who was standing somewhere behind those brick-layered walls. His mother made this day happen for him. And he would be forever grateful to her for it.

"Are you sure about this, honey?" Karma asked, stroking the back of his neck.

Mekhi turned and faced his mother, staring back at her lovingly. "Yeah, Ma. I'm sure."

"All right." Karma smiled, rubbing his cheek with the back of her hand. "Let's go then."

Mother and son unlocked their seatbelts, opened their doors and exited the vehicle. They walked toward the sidewalk, then up the gray concrete stairway to the glass doors that led into the large carpeted foyer. Karma looked around the massive room for Money, finally spotting him at one of the ticket service desks across the way.

"There he is," she said to Mekhi in a hushed tone.

She and Mekhi began to make their way over to him just as he was turning around to meet their eyes with his.

"Hey." Money smiled, taken by Karma's beauty once again.

"Hey, yourself," she replied nervously, noticing he cut his beard down to a thick goatee.

She looked over at Mekhi, taking his hand into hers and squeezing it. She lightly pulled him forward and exhaled.

"Well, here he is." She smiled. "Here's your son."

Money stepped back, folded his hands at his thighs, and shook his head in disbelief. He couldn't believe his eyes. It was as if he'd given birth to Mekhi himself. If it wasn't for his mother's markings in his eyes and his hair texture, his brows and chiseled jawline, she wouldn't have been able to claim him as her own.

"Let me look at you, man," he mustered.

Mekhi stood before his father with his hands in his pockets and his head tilted back. He towered over the man who almost took his life. It was almost surreal to stare back into the face that favored his so much.

"You're beautiful," Money admitted with tears in his eyes.

"Thank you." Mekhi blushed in embarrassment.

"You've done one helluva job, Karm," Money declared, fighting back his

tears. "Look at him. This is our boy."

"Yes, it is," Karma agreed.

A prideful smile spread across Money's face. He couldn't take his eyes off of Mekhi.

"You guys should go on and get your condiments. The movie's going to start soon, isn't it?" Karma asked in an attempt to break up the awkwardness between them.

"Yeah, yeah, it is," Money replied, finally pulling his eyes away from their son. "You ready, son?"

"Yeah," Mekhi replied with a nod.

"All right, then." Money smiled. "Hey, Karm," he began, taking her hands into his. "Thanks again for this." He kissed her on the cheek.

"You're welcome." She flinched. Gently, she took her

hands out of Money's grasp and walked up to Mekhi.

"If you need me, call me. I'll be right across the street in the mall," she explained in a serious tone.

"Okay," he confirmed.

"I love you," Karma whispered.

"Love you, too, Ma," Mekhi replied.

"Okay, I'll see you later," she replied, composing herself. Karma pulled Mekhi's face toward hers and kissed him on the cheek.

"Enjoy." She waved good-bye to Money and walked out of the theatre.

Father and son watched the most important woman in their lives sashay down the concrete stairway, onto the sidewalk and toward her car. Mekhi managed to take his eyes off her first. He looked over at his father and studied his steady gaze. There was longing and love there. He didn't know much about lost love, but he knew his father made his mother uncomfortable with that stare. She could barely hold his gaze without blushing or briefly turning away. He made her uncomfortable . . . nervous. Maybe she still loved him. Mekhi wasn't sure, but he'd ask her as soon as the business he had with his father was taken care of.

"I don't think this was a good idea," Indigo said. "What if he tries to kill him again?" Karma and Indigo sat in a booth at TGIF's waiting for their meals to arrive. Indigo took her straw and twirled the ice in her large glass of Sprite while Karma watched her.

"I highly doubt he's going to try to kill him at the movies." Karma sighed.

"I mean *in general*, Karma," Indigo spat smugly.

"I was being facetious, Indigo. Damn."

"You should have left his behind right at Shoprite where you found him."

"Well, I didn't."

A loud silence ensued.

"What time are you going back over to pick him up?" Indigo asked.

"Whenever he calls me," Karma replied.

"Oh." Indigo exhaled.

"You know, I didn't have to tell you," Karma confessed.

"Well, I really wish you hadn't," Indigo said.

The two locked eyes.

"If *Tio* or Stuff finds out . . ." Indigo said.

"Well, the only way they'll find out is if you tell them. You know, just like the time you told them Money raped me after I asked you not to?" Karma stated.

Silence fell between the two.

"How long are you going to hold that against me?" Indigo asked, trying to compose herself.

"Please, I let that go years ago. I'm just simply refreshing your memory," Karma replied, as she took the cherry out of her vanilla milkshake and popped it in her mouth. "Besides, *Tio's* up in age now. He doesn't need to get involved in something like this."

"Because you know he'll be disappointed in you," Indigo stated.

"What?" Karma asked.

"You heard me. You know he'll give you the third degree for letting that man back into your life."

"Let's get one thing straight. He is *not* back in my life. He's back in Mekhi's, okay?" Karma corrected her.

"If you say so." Indigo rolled her eyes.

"What the fuck is that supposed to mean?"

"What do you think it means?"

"You know, you've been questioning my judgment for months. From the time I kicked Mekhi out, to my relationship with Hassan, and now this. I didn't question you about how you dealt with Desiree after we found out she was fuckin', or your relationship with Stuff and his lies."

"His lies?" Indigo queried.

"Yes, *his lies*. He killed Curtis, Indigo. No matter how many times or how many different ways he tells you he didn't. *He did.* He killed him."

Indigo looked away, then met her cousin's eyes again. "He closed the chapter on that part of his life a long time ago. He hasn't killed anyone in years."

Karma pursed her lips in disgust. "The kids may not know anything about our past . . . Stuff and me. But they know enough about our present to never question what we're possibly capable of."

Indigo stared back at her stone-faced cousin.

Chapter 25

"Your sister told me these last two years have been rough for you and your mother," Money said as he placed a forkful of chicken and broccoli in his mouth.

"You can say dat," Mekhi admitted, taking a bite out of his soft shell taco.

"You wanna tell me how?" Money took a sip of water from his plastic bottle.

"I gotta bad temper. So does she," Mekhi said, taking another bite out of his taco.

Money watched him closely. "Taco good?"

"Mm-hmm," Mekhi replied, wiping his mouth with a napkin.

Money chuckled to himself. "You know, you get your temper from the both of us."

"Is dat how you ended up tryin' to kill me? Ya temper got da best of you?" Mekhi asked, holding his father's gaze.

"Yes." Money nodded.

"But I didn't do anything to you. I was only a baby," Mekhi said matter-of-factly.

"That's right. You were." Money nodded again.

"Den, why?" Mekhi asked, sitting back in his chair. "What pissed you off so bad dat you went after *me?*"

"Did your grandmother tell you anything about your grandfather? My father?" Money inquired.

"Are you gonna answer my question?" Mekhi replied, agitated.

"Just as soon as you answer mine," Money said.

Mekhi shrugged and shook his head in disbelief.

"Well?" Money went on.

"Da one time I asked about him, she told me he was a cruel man who hurt her in every way imaginable. Dat she still wore da scars . . . or somethin' like dat. But I never saw 'em. She never showed 'em to me," Mekhi said.

"Your grandmother was right. He was a cruel man. He used to beat her in his many rages, almost killing her a couple of times. He was a monster. And that's why I tried to take your life, son. That rage that he had, lived inside of me, and I saw that you possessed it as well. I saw it in you when you were just an infant. Your mother and I had broken up. It was a nasty split. One emotion turned into another, and I eventually snapped. I just . . . snapped. And in my ill state of mind, I—" Money paused. Tears welled up in his eyes. He tried to blink them back, but they would not retreat. "I put a .380 caliber to your back and, uh, pulled the trigger. I couldn't bear the thought of my son living the rest of his life with the blood of Jimmy Hayes coursing through his veins."

"Den you should have wrapped ya shit up when you ran up in my mother," Mekhi said slowly.

"Hey, now, let's not get disrespectful, all right?" Money warned with a wary grin.

"Is it true dat she found you in my room sittin' in her rockin' chair wit' da gun still in ya hand?"

"Yes," Money replied.

"And she found me in da crib bleedin' out?" Mekhi pressed.

"Yes," Money said.

"Did she really run all da way to University wit' me in her arms?" Mekhi queried.

"Barefoot," Money professed.

In that very moment, Mekhi wished he'd listened to his mother and not had this meeting with his killer. He was satisfied, more so now than ever, to have called and considered Master Sergeant Lorenzo Walker his father. He wanted nothing more to do with this man. He'd given him a poor excuse for the attempt on his life. As far as Mekhi was concerned, there was no justification for his actions. He didn't care how nasty the break-up was between his parents, no real man would punish the woman he supposedly loved by killing their child.

"Did you ever put ya hands on my mother?" Mekhi asked.

"Never," Money replied honestly.

"Call her out of her name?"

"A few times," Money admitted.

Mekhi laughed in disbelief. "You know, she's neva missed a meet? Not a swim or a track meet. She's neva missed one. *Not one.* No matter how many fights we've had over da years. No matter how much I've disrespected her. She's always *there*." He nodded. "She's da one who put me in da water. *Cured me* of my back spasms. Shit's so bad, dey took my breath away."

Money shifted in his seat.

"I've spent da last sixteen years blamin' her for your absence. Takin' my anger towards you, out on her," Mekhi said, shaking his head in disdain. "Puttin' my hands on her and shit. She almost died because of me. Did you know dat? Right before Thanksgivin'. She took a whole bottle of pills to da head and went to sleep. Mimi tell you?"

"Yes," Money answered.

"Yeah, dis is da type of shit I'm carryin' wit' me. It's crazy, because I used to pray to God every night for dis day. *Every* night . . . wishin' for *you, dreamin'* about you. Always thinkin' about what you were like, what we had in common, if I really looked like you, if you were really da good guy my grandmother made you out to be. But now I know she wasn't goin' to say anything bad about you, because you were her son. Right or wrong, she was in your corner 'til the very end. *Your father's touched, baby*, dat's what she always said. But I know better, now. You knew exactly what you were doin', and you had everybody fooled. Mimi's still fooled."

"Are you finished?" Money asked haughtily.

"No. I just have one more thing to say," Mekhi said. "I'm ashamed to be ya son, 'cause you ain't shit."

Unexpectedly, Money jumped up from his seat and grabbed

Mekhi by his coat collar. He pulled the teen's body halfway across the table and violently shook him. Their trays of food and beverages went crashing to the floor. Patrons sitting near them rose from their seats and cried out for help. Mekhi wrapped his hands around his father's throat and squeezed it with all his might. Money released his right hand from Mekhi's collar, balled it into a fist and struck him in the face. Mekhi released his father's neck and placed his hands over his throbbing jaw. Money lunged at the boy again, taking a good amount of his coat and shirt into his hands and began dragging him out of the food court and into the shopping area. Father and son threw solid punches at each other, countless blows connecting to the face and body.

A crowd soon formed around them, capturing the attention of Indigo and Karma, who were stepping out of The Body Shop across the way. Karma caught a glimpse of her son as he fell brutally to the floor. She dropped her bags and ran over to the brawl, pushing her way through the crowd. Indigo picked up her cousin's bags and followed suit. Two heavy-set Hispanic men struggled to restrain Money. Karma ran to Mekhi's side and took in the damage done to his face. He had a nasty cut under his left eye, and his mouth was once again, torn open. His shirt was ripped and stained with blood. She helped him stagger to his feet, before turning toward Money, charging at him and assaulting him with wild slaps and punches. One of the Hispanic men left Money's side and pulled her away with Mekhi and Indigo's assistance.

"You're dead, Money! Dead!" Karma screamed.

"Karma, stop, stop, stop!" Indigo begged.

"Dead, muthafucka!"

Chapter 26

It had been a long evening, the majority of it spent in the emergency room. Karma yawned as she pulled up to one of the gates for American Airlines at Newark Liberty Airport. Money had done a number on Mekhi. He needed stitches for the gash under his eye and on his bottom lip. Karma and the appointed physician decided the use of a skin adhesive would be a better choice than sutures, because it left little to no scarring once the wounds healed. Money had also fractured four of the boy's ribs.

Once mother and son arrived home, Mekhi asked her if she could make the couch into a bed. An attempt to climb the stairs would be a great defeat. Karma obliged. Within seconds of his head hitting his pillow, Mekhi fell into a deep, medicated slumber. Karma kissed him gently on the forehead before heading out the door to pick Hassan up from the airport.

Karma put the car in park, turned the hazard lights on, and then stepped out into the frigid night air. She walked around to the passenger side and leaned against the door, folding her arms across her chest.

Hassan walked through the automatic sliding doors and smiled at the sight of his woman. "Hey, beautiful," he said, wrapping his arms around her waist.

"Hey, baby," she replied, tiredly .

He bent down and kissed her lovingly on the lips. "Mmm," he groaned in delight before kissing her again.

Karma slipped the tip of her tongue into his mouth, then slowly pulled away, smiling.

"Mmm," he grunted again, shaking his head. "Want me to drive?"

"Please," she replied.

"All right. Hand 'em over," Hassan teased, with his massive hand out. Karma placed the keys in it.

Stepping forward, Hassan opened the passenger door and Karma got in. He then popped the trunk and threw his luggage inside. Once Hassan entered the warmth of the vehicle, he turned the hazard lights off and sped off down the terminal.

"How was your flight?" Karma asked in a yawn. "Excuse me."

"So, does that mean there's no chance of me gettin' any tonight?" Hassan grinned.

Karma gave him a stern look, her lips pursed.

Hassan chuckled to himself. "I'm just kidding, baby. I really don't know how the flight was. I slept through it."

"You're a mess," Karma said, shaking her head.

"Yeah, I know," he agreed. "Now, tell me about this fight Mekhi had today. He all right?"

Hassan had called when she and Mekhi were at the

hospital, and Karma explained in little detail, why they were there. She'd promised that she'd fill him in, completely, once he returned to Jersey.

"No, he's not," she admitted shamefully.

"Well, tell me about it," he insisted.

"I'd rather tell you when we get home."

"It's that bad?" Hassan looked over at her briefly.

"Mm-hmm."

"Damn."

"Yeah." Karma sighed. "Do you mind if we make a pit stop on our way home?" Karma yawned again. "My uncle asked me to drop by."

"No, I don't mind," Hassan assured her as he switched lanes.

"Okay. Thank you." She smiled, closing her eyes.

Karma turned the doorknob to her uncle's condo and stepped into the short hallway leading to the living room. Hassan closed the door behind them. They made their way into the room where Miguel, Maggie, Indigo and Stuff awaited. Curious, Karma met each one of their eyes. She struggled to read everyone's face, except that of Indigo's. A mixture of qualm and compunction showed themselves clearly. She bit down on her bottom lip, then looked back at Hassan in disbelief.

"What the hell is this?" Karma queried, crossing her arms.

"Sit down, *amado*," Miguel asked in a non-threatening tone.

"No, thank you. I'd rather stand," she replied curtly.

"Karma," he restated firmly.

"It came down to this, Indigo? Really? Stuff? *Tia?*" Karma sneered.

"Karma!" Miguel hollered, sitting erect in his chair.

"What?" Karma snapped her head in his direction.

"Sit," Miguel restated.

For a moment Karma stood before obliging.

"You as well, Señor Turner," Miguel continued, folding his hands in his lap. Hassan did so. Miguel turned his attention back to his agitated niece.

"Indigo and Stuff informed your aunt and me that you allowed *loco loco* to meet with Mekhi earlier today. And it went awry. Is that correct?"

Karma stared back at Indigo and Stuff without batting her eyes. Indigo, uneasy under her gaze, quickly looked away.

"*Tio—*"

"Yes or no will suffice," Miguel countered tersely.

"Yes." Karma gulped.

"He almost killed him—again," he professed, his aged eyes fixed in a squint.

"Yes," Karma replied with glossy eyes.

Hassan rubbed his hand over his goatee as he watched the love of his life begin to unravel under her uncle's interrogation. He knew how close the two were. Miguel stepped into her father's place when the soldier was away on his tours of duty.

"What were you thinking?" Miguel asked, shifting angrily in his chair. "What!"

In response, Karma shook her head. Tears rolled down her cheeks.

"*Me responde!*" Miguel roared.

"I did it for Mekhi," she whimpered. "It's what he wanted."

"But did he *need* it?" he refuted, leaning forward.

"Yes, *Tio*. Yes." "He needed to see what I've been trying to tell him all along. What we've all told him about his father over the years," Karma cried.

"You didn't protect him, Karma."

"What?" she asked, perplexed.

"You didn't protect him," he uttered again.

"Don't say that, *Tio*," Karma begged.

"You didn't."

Maggie moved to the edge of her seat and held her hands up in submission. "All right, now. Wait a minute." Things were getting way out of hand. Even though she didn't agree with Karma's decision, she thought Miguel's judgment of her, in particular, was too critical.

"No woman . . . no *mother* . . . in her right mind would allow her son to meet with the man who tried to take his life," Miguel emphasized, with the twitch of his injured hand.

"Whoa, unc'," Stuff chimed in.

"*Tio*," Indigo whispered at the same time.

"How can you say that to me?" Karma jumped up, screaming at the top of her lungs. "I'm a good mother! I'm a good mother!"

"Karma," Indigo and Maggie called, running over to her.

"You never accused my mother of being unfit after she had me arrested for assaulting Jimmy's ass! Trying to save her from being raped and shit!" Karma bawled. "It didn't work, but I tried. Goddamnit! I tried!"

Hassan gently grabbed her wrist and wrapped his arm around her waist. He pulled her into him, resting his head against hers. "Baby, baby," he whispered in her ear.

"Did that make her a bad mother?" Karma continued.

"Yes." Miguel nodded slowly.

"No, it didn't! No, it didn't!" Karma howled. "She did it out of fear! All I did today was let my son go! Just this once to show him that he's better off without his father! He's always been better off without him!" Karma sniffled as her heart began to go numb. "And you know what? You know what he did? He fought back—and then he thanked me for it." Karma wiped her running nose with the back of her hand, before pulling away from Maggie, Indigo, and Hassan.

"And since you're in the questioning mood tonight, *Tio*. Criticizing my parenting skills. Why don't you ask Indigo and Stuff about Desi's baby daddy," Karma spat, straight-faced.

Turning her back, Karma walked toward the door. She opened it and stormed out.

"You okay?" Hassan asked sincerely, after leaning forward and looking up at Karma as he rested his arms in his lap. He folded his hands as he shifted his weight on the edge of the bed.

Afraid that she would try to commit suicide again, Hassan decided he would approach the discussion of the day's events cautiously. He didn't want to upset Karma anymore. She was in a fragile state.

"No." Karma shook her head, sniffling back tears.

"I don't agree with the way your family approached you tonight," Hassan confessed. And he didn't. He also didn't agree with Karma's allowance of the meeting between Money and Mekhi. He didn't appreciate her keeping it from her family or him. But he understood. He saw that tonight. And Hassan didn't want to be on the offense.

"But your uncle was right. He could have killed him," he said in an even tone.

"I know," Karma admitted, just above a whisper.

"And I don't think it was right that Mekhi blackmailed you the way he did. He knows how much you love me, and he used it in his favor. That wasn't right. You should have called me, love. And we should have come to an agreement about how to approach this situation properly. You and I.

Together."

"I agree with everything you're saying. I was wrong. Mekhi was wrong," she professed.

"Is there anything else I should know?"

"Like what?"

"Like, were there any other *meetings* between you and this lunatic that I should know about?"

"Are you asking me if I've been unfaithful?"

"Yeah. I am," he said quietly.

"I can't believe you."

"I asked you to be my *wife*, Karma."

"And I told you I would accept upon my children's blessing," Karma replied, her eyes turning dark.

"How can I trust you after this? You tell me. How?" he asked, sitting erectly.

Karma stood before him, her eyes locked with his. Hassan was not the insecure type. And she felt awful for making him feel that way, but he knew the history between her and Money was a terrible one. And Karma felt he should have known better than to insinuate that she would bed him again. Even if she did have that incident with Money in the Don Pepe restroom.

"How can you sit there and suggest that I slept with him? I mean, if you want to get down and dirty, I guess I should be asking you the same question. Is there anything *I* should know? Are you fuckin' anyone out there in LA?" Karma spat.

"No, I'm not," Hassan said, shaking his head.

"And how do I know you're telling the truth? I don't," she answered for him. "I can only go by what you tell me. And *trust* your word." Karma moved toward him, kneeling down at his feet. "I'm too old and too secure to hire a private detective to follow you around out there." She grinned. "You have nothing to worry about, baby. I'm all yours. And I'm sorry for lying to you and making you question us. What can I do to make it right?" Karma asked, seducing him with her golden eyes.

"I don't know," Hassan admitted forlornly.

"No?" Karma rubbed his thighs.

"No." He tried to compose himself. Her touch was like kryptonite.

"Are you sure?" She licked her lips and unbuttoned his pants, her gaze never wavering.

"No," Hassan said. He pinched his nose in anticipation.

Karma smiled. She reached into his boxers and pulled his manhood out. Pleased to see that it was ready and waiting for her. She took him into her mouth and made Hassan forget Money even existed.

Chapter 27

"Why don't you and Stuff consider letting she have the baby, then give it up for adoption?" Maggie suggested as she prepared her morning coffee. "Her not ready for dis procedure, Indigo."

"Yeah, well, she wasn't ready to lay down with that boy either, but she did," Indigo countered. Maggie sucked her teeth long and hard.

"She's lucky I didn't beat it out of her," Indigo sneered.

"You were close," Maggie admitted, locking eyes with her. "Reconsider. The baby is innocent."

Indigo couldn't believe what she was hearing. Her mother was as strict as a West Indian mother came. She didn't allow her to do anything growing up. It was all about school, dance, chores and church . . . nothing else. If she'd gotten pregnant by Stuff in her teens, Desi would have been a huge blood clot on the floor.

"Until it grows into a Desiree," she snapped. Indigo had no remorse for her child. Desiree had betrayed her trust. She didn't think she kept her so close that the girl didn't feel she could ever come to her about anything. But maybe she had. They had "the talk" more times than she could remember, and Desi swore that she would wait until she was an adult to engage in any sexual activity. Maybe she and Stuff should have allowed her to date Curtis. Maybe then they wouldn't be in this predicament.

Maggie shook her head in dismay. "Me never knew you could be so cruel."

"Me either," Indigo professed with tears in her eyes. She turned and walked out of the kitchen. Making her way to the second floor to wake Desi. Her bedroom door was closed. Indigo placed her hand on the knob and turned it. She pushed the door open and stormed into the room.

Empty. Desi's bed was empty. Indigo travelled to the bathroom connected to the room with hurried steps. She wasn't in there. Indigo jogged into the hallway and began to check every room and closet.

"Desi!" she called. "Desi!"

"What's going on?" Maggie yelled from the bottom of the stairwell.

"Desi's gone!" Indigo replied, descending the steps.

"What you mean *gone?*" Maggie asked, perplexed.

"She's not in the house, Mommy! She's gone!" Indigo screamed in frustration.

"Where?" Maggie questioned, on Indigo's heels.

"I don't know, Mommy. I don't know," Indigo huffed as she paced back and forth in the living room and searched for any clues, like a note or something that would assist her in this quest to find her daughter.

She reached into her pocket and retrieved her cell phone. She dialed Desi's number.

"Hi, this is Desi," the voice recording began. "I'm unable to answer your call right now, so please leave your name, number, and a message after the tone. And I'll get back to you as soon as I can!"

An alert tone chimed thereafter. "Desi, this is Mommy. Call me as soon as you get this." Indigo pressed the END icon on the screen. "Shit!"

"What?" Maggie asked, rubbing her arms nervously.

"She turned her phone off," Indigo informed her. She began scrolling through her contacts, falling upon Karma's number. She pressed it and waited for her to pick up.

"Hello?" Karma breathed into the receiver.

"*Prima*, have you seen Desi? Is she with you?" Indigo asked, hoping Karma was going to say 'yes.'

"No. Why? What's the matter?" Karma asked with alarm.

"She's missing. I think she ran away. I don't . . . I don't know," Indigo replied, rubbing her forehead.

"What?" Karma sat straight up. "Wait, hold on for a minute. Let me go ask Mekhi if he's heard from her."

"Okay." Indigo paced.

"What her say?" Maggie began, before Indigo waved her hand to silence her.

"*Prima?*" Karma said.

"Yeah." Indigo paused, holding her breath.

"He said he hasn't heard from her."

Indigo's heart dropped. "Can you . . . can you come

over, please?" she heard herself say in a shiver.

"I'm on my way." Karma disconnected the call.

"Mommy?" Indigo whimpered, swaying a little. She reached for her. Maggie grabbed her hand and guided her to the couch.

"Me here, me here. Come, have a seat," she urged.

"Call Stuff." Indigo exhaled, her eyes closed.

"Okay, okay. Lay back," Maggie instructed, before snatching the phone from Indigo's hand and jumping up from the couch.

She found her place back in the kitchen. Stuff's phone rang three times before he finally picked up.

"Wassup, baby?" he answered in a cheerful tone.

"Got you the bendable straws, man," Carmine said as he entered Mekhi's house.

"'Preciate it," Mekhi replied, receiving the straws from Carmine's hand. He closed the door behind him. The duo made their way into the living room and sat down on the couch.

"Ya moms drop you off?" Mekhi asked with a cotton-filled mouth.

"Nah, I rode my bike." Carmine shrugged.

"You put it in da back, right?" Mekhi uttered with furrowed brows.

"Yeah, of course. Now, more importantly . . . how you feelin'?" Carmine removed his leather motocross jacket and laid it on the arm of the accent chair nearby.

"Still sore as shit," Mekhi proclaimed.

"Well, you look good," Carmine admitted. "Swelling's gone down a lot."

"Yeah." Mekhi nodded.

"How's your mom? She still beatin' herself up over it?" Carmine asked.

"Not as much. Had a long talk wit' her and Turner da otha night," Mekhi confessed. "He's helpin' her to move on from it."

"And how do you feel about that?" Carmine queried.

"I mean, dat's her man, her fiancé or whateva, so he's doin' what he's supposed to do." He shrugged.

"You gave 'em your blessing?" Carmine grinned.

"She deserves to be happy. And he makes her happy." Mekhi smirked.

"That's what's up, Khi. I'm proud of you, man."

"Thanks, man. Turner's a cool dude. Gotta lotta heart. He calls to check on me. Shit like dat." Mekhi nodded.

"I told you. Never block your blessings, man. You may have lost your

grandfather, but look at the gift he left behind for you." Carmine nudged Mekhi gently in the arm.

"Trillz." Mekhi smiled.

"So, what else is new?" Carmine continued.

"Desi's missin'." Mekhi stared him dead in the eyes.

"What?" !" Carmine placed his head in his hands.

"Da fam's out lookin' for her now. Mekhi clenched his jaw. "She was supposed to get an abortion today . . . dis mornin'. But when my aunt went to wake her up, she wasn't in her bed. Nowhere in da house."

"Where do you think she is?" Carmine asked, his face strained with worry.

"I don't know. She could be anywhere. She could be here, she could be over in da city. Travelin' ain't nothin' to her. She saves her allowance, so where eva she is, she got money in her pockets. I don't know. I just . . . I don't know. My aunt used to be a cop, so every precinct in Jersey is on alert. Even da state troopers know about her disappearance."

"But they can't do anything until twenty-four hours have passed." Carmine thought aloud.

"Nope. Dey sure can't," Mekhi agreed.

"Damn." Carmine shook his head. "You reach out to Ekua?"

"Yeah, she hasn't heard from her either." Mekhi sighed.

"Wow. And how's that goin'?" Carmine queried.

"I mean, I haven't really spoken to her. Not on some 'gimme anotha chance' type shit. Today was da first time we talked in weeks. And it was brief as hell," Mekhi confessed.

The doorbell rang. The boys looked toward the door, then at each other warily. Mekhi rose from the couch, making his way to the foyer. He looked through the stained glass window embedded in the door and sighed. Opening it, thereafter. Ekua looked up at him with tears in her eyes.

Mekhi let his guard down and reached for her. He took her by the hand, pulling her into him. She buried her face into his stomach and wrapped her arms around his muscular frame. Mekhi, in turn, did the same. Ekua felt safe there. In his arms. And Mekhi didn't mind being her saviour. It just felt so right.

"I'm scared," Ekua whispered, lying beneath Mekhi in all her nude glory. She covered her breasts with her hands.

"Don't be. I'll be gentle. I promise," Mekhi assured her. He slowly unfolded her arms and placed them around his neck. He leaned in and kissed her tenderly. He massaged her young breasts with the palm of his hand, then took them into his warm mouth. Mekhi could feel Ekua stiffen beneath him, so he moved his tongue between her breasts, down to her navel, then to the garden between her sculpted legs. She gasped when he put his lips to hers. The skillfulness of his tongue sent shock waves through her virginal body. Mekhi gripped her hips tightly, devouring her sweet nectar. He rose and fell with her hips as she held on to his head and whimpered in pleasure. Mekhi knew he had her where he wanted her. He crawled back on top of her and kissed her again. He took his throbbing member into his hand and aligned it with her vaginal opening. Gradually, he moved forward, squeezing through her tightness. He cursed to himself as Ekua gasped, her eyes fluttering upon his excruciating entrance. Tears formed in her eyes as pain surged through her. Her body tensed again.

"It hurts," she cried in Mekhi's ear.

"I'm sorry," he moaned. "I just need to . . . damn, baby."

Ekua dug her fingernails into his back. She tried to relax, but couldn't. Her insides were on fire. Mekhi was taking his time and being as gentle as he could, but it seemed as if her hymen had plans of its own. Not to give way.

"Try to relax," he whispered into her neck. Ekua winced in pain, squirming beneath him.

Mekhi licked his fingers, then placed them on her clitoris. He massaged it in a slow, circular motion. The two locked eyes and gradually, Ekua relaxed. Mekhi went back and forth between stimulating her with his fingers and his penis. He kissed and nibbled the erogenous zone on her neck; she moaned in ecstasy. Then, it happened. The gateway to her secret garden gave way. Their hips were suddenly joined, uniting them as one. That moment----necessary for the both of them. One of comfort and an escape from their harsh reality.

Chapter 28

"You have to try to get some sleep, *prima*," Karma said into her Bluetooth earpiece. She was in the process of closing *Soleil's* for the night. Karma snapped her fingers to get the attention of two of her busboys. She questioned them about an overflowing bus pan hidden underneath the bar with her hands. Each blamed the other for the oversight. She held her hand in midair, shaking her head.

"I don't care. Get it out of here," she mouthed.

The young men picked the heavy basin up and scurried to the kitchen.

"I can't. I won't be able to sleep until she's home." Indigo sniffled.

"I know, I know." Karma sighed with tears brimming in her eyes.

"Are you coming over?" Indigo asked in a small voice.

"Yes, honey. I'll be right over after I go home and check on Mekhi," Karma replied, traveling through the dining hall.

"Okay," Indigo said sadly.

It was a quarter after midnight. Seventeen hours had already passed, and Desiree was still nowhere to be found.

Indigo had been an absolute mess and wanted nothing more than her cousin's company.

"Is Stuff still out?" Karma asked, already knowing the answer.

"Mm-hmm." Indigo sighed.

Karma shook her head. When she saw Stuff earlier that day, he was beside himself. He'd come home to two hysterical women. Both inconsolable. He'd been unable to get anything out of them, so he turned to Karma. He immediately rallied a number of local drug dealers and asked them to patrol the streets. He and Karma explored the ins and outs of Essex County, the beginnings and ends of Harlem, Midtown, and the Village, to no avail. The Arts High School staff and student body were on high alert. Everyone in prayer.

Eight o'clock couldn't come soon enough. It wouldn't be until then that they could officially file a missing person's report.

"Where's *Tia*?" Karma queried, entering the kitchen.

"She's asleep," Indigo replied.

Karma walked around the space, making sure it was clean and everything was in its rightful place. She gave the kitchen and maintenance staff a thumbs up. Then the 'OK' to go.

"Very nice. Thank you," she mouthed.

Karma made her way to her office thereafter, cutting the lights off in the dining hall, bar, and lounge on the way there. She grabbed her scarf and tied it around her neck, then her coat off the coat rack.

"Do you want me to pick up anything on my way over?" she asked, zipping her coat.

"No. I just want you," Indigo cried.

"All right. Don't cry, honey." Karma sighed.

"I can't help it."

"I know. Everything's going to be okay. Just hold on for me. Okay?" Karma begged. "I'm on my way."

"Okay." Indigo hiccupped.

"Bye." Karma disconnected the call. She shut down her office for the evening, then turned on the security system. She stepped out into the cold, and upon seeing a dark shadow, Karma jumped and let out a high shriek. She clutched her chest, then placed her hand on her forehead.

"What the hell are you doing?" she asked.

"I didn't mean to scare you. I just want to talk to you," Money said, shifting his weight to one foot.

"We have nothing to talk about, Money," Karma hissed, trying to move past him. He blocked her.

"Move," she said, trying to bypass him.

"Is Mekhi all right?" Money asked sincerely.

Karma shook her head and attempted to side step him once again.

"Karma." Money moved in her space.

"Get the fuck out of my way, Money!"

"No. Not until you tell me if he's all right or not," he replied, his eyes pleading.

"No, he's not all right! He's *never* been all right!"

"I didn't mean to hit 'im."

"Well, trust and believe you won't get the opportunity to do it again," she replied smugly, pushing past him.

Money grabbed her arm and held it tight. "Wait a minute!"

Karma looked at his hand on her arm, then back at him. "Get the fuck off of me!"

"No. I'm not finished talkin' to you!"

"Let go of me, Money!" she demanded, trying to tug her arm from his grasp.

"No. I gotta make things right between us. Between me and Mekhi." He squeezed her arm tighter.

Karma locked eyes with Money and saw it—that crazed look in his eyes. The same look he had the night he put his gun to Mekhi's back. A chill ran up her spine.

"You're hurting me," she said carefully, wincing in pain.

"Let me fix things. I love you, Karma. I love Mekhi. Give me another chance," he begged. "Please?"

"No . . . Money."

"Why not?" he barked, tightening his grip.

"Let go of me!"

"Why can't you just admit that you still love me?"

"Because I don't!"

"Well, your pussy told me different."

"What happened at Don Pepe's was a mistake. That

should have never happened."

"That wasn't a mistake, Karm," he replied, intensely. "You can't tell me the electricity you felt between us wasn't real."

"Whatever that was—that energy—it was wrong and misguided. My heart *and* my pussy belong to someone else. Now, let go of me!"

"No." Money tightened his grip.

The two began to tussle. Karma tried her hardest to pry his hand from her arm. Money grabbed her other arm and shook her violently. Their voices rose, waking a number of sleeping residents in the apartment buildings behind the lot. Lights came on. Concerned faces emerged in windows.

A black Infiniti pulled into the parking lot, parking haphazardly in a space. Hassan jumped out and dashed over to the quarrelling couple. He ran behind Money and locked his head in the crux of his arm. He placed his hand on his head and held it steady.

Money immediately let go of Karma. In a panic, he grabbed Hassan's arm and tried to pull it away from his neck. He couldn't breathe. His windpipe was being crushed.

"Go to sleep!" Hassan howled.

"Hassan!" Karma yelled.

"Go to sleep, bitch!" he growled again.

Karma scampered over to the man of her past and the man of her present and future, and attempted to loosen Hassan's vise grip. Not because she wanted to save Money, but to keep Hassan out of prison for murder.

"Hassan! Let him go!" she shouted, tugging at his arm. "Hassan! Has-san!"

"What!" He looked over at the love of his life, his nostrils flaring. Lips tight.

"Let him go!" Karma stressed.

Hassan released him, brutally shoving him to the ground.

"You all right?" he asked, taking her face into his hands.

"Mm-hmm," she replied, visibly shaken.

Money leaped to his feet and rushed the former running back. The two fell onto the hood of Hassan's car. Hassan punched Money repeatedly in the back before Money gained his footing and flung Hassan to the ground. He pounced on him. The blows to Hassan's face were hard and vicious. Hassan grabbed Money by the collar of his coat and unexpectedly head-butted him twice. The second blow sent Money falling backward, holding his nose. A river of blood seeped through his fingers.

Karma jogged to Hassan's side and helped him to his feet. He grabbed his jaw, moving it from one side to the other.

"Bitch!" he screamed, kicking Money in the stomach.

"Stop, Hassan!" Karma pleaded, pulling him away.

"Touch her or that boy again and I'll kill you, nigga!" he promised, hovering over him. "You hear me, bitch? They're mine!" Hassan hissed.

Sirens sounded in the distance.

"Baby, please? We have to go," Karma urged, pushing him toward his car.

"Mine!" he roared.

Hassan and Karma jumped into his car and sped away. Money lay, writhing in pain. His nose, spirit, and heart—broken. He may have lost the battle, but the war was far from over.

Chapter 29

MISSING ORANGE TEENAGER FOUND IN THE NEWARK BAY

By Robert Napier/*The Star-Ledger*
December 19, 2017

The body of a fair-skinned female found in an open field in the Richard A. Rutkowski Park in Bayonne has been identified as Desiree Davis, 17, of Orange. A couple made the gruesome discovery yesterday evening.

The county prosecutor's office said Davis, whose remains and clothing were drenched, may have jumped or been pushed off of the Newark Bay Bridge, (officially known as the Vincent R. Casciano Memorial Bridge), and drowned. She was reported missing by her family over a week ago. Davis was last seen by her parents last Sunday evening at their home. Davis, a junior at Newark's Arts High School, was a gifted dancer who was in preparation for auditioning for the Alvin Ailey Pre-Professional Program in New York City.

"Desiree was one of our best and brightest stars," Kurtrina Holloway, principal of Arts High, said. "We're

absolutely heartbroken."

Holloway said next month's winter dance program will be dedicated to the late teenager.

Word of Davis's disappearance spread rapidly through her hometown. Business owners and residents joined forces with the police and fire departments, taking to the streets in search of her.

"I have a granddaughter her age," Orange Fire Captain Gerard Long said. "It could have been her. It was only right for us to come together as a community and look for one of our children."

The Medical Examiner has not determined the cause or manner of death . Autopsy results by the Regional Medical Examiner's Office are still pending.

Karma held Indigo's hair back as she vomited her insufferable grief in the toilet. They'd just returned from identifying Desi's body at the ME's Office. Karma could still smell the decomposition from all the unclaimed bodies. She sobbed as her mind played back the moment of Desi's unveiling. She stood on one side of Indigo, while Stuff stood on the other. Both of them with an arm around her waist. Poor Indigo collapsed the moment Desi's face was revealed from under the white sheet she lay under. An animal-like howl escaped from Stuff as he cradled his fallen wife in his arms.

Karma became light-headed. The ME asked her to confirm if it was their beloved baby girl. And she did, but not without mentally questioning why their reaction wasn't enough verification. She couldn't deny the red curly hair or the nose and lips the girl shared with her father. And even though her skin was ashen and her face, eaten away in some places, it was indeed Desi.

Indigo eventually regained consciousness. Two security guards assisted Karma with the devastated parents, escorting them all back to her truck. The drive home took longer than it should have. Indigo screamed the entire way, causing Karma to run a red light and get pulled over by a police officer. Once she explained the absentminded act, he escorted them home. Sirens blaring.

Now, here they were on Indigo's bathroom floor— broken. Karma wiped her burning eyes and running nose with her shirtsleeve. Fourteen years ago she was almost in Indigo's position, but God had spared her child. She wiped the sweat from Indigo's forehead. There was no way to console her. So she didn't try.

Karma shook her head in an attempt to bury the wails coming from the floor below them. The entire family was downstairs drowning in a sea of tears. Karma could hear her aunt keening, and knew she was holding her arms outstretched to the sky. Her uncle screamed to the heavens in Spanish, cursing God for allowing such a thing to happen to one of his angels.

This storm was too great. She didn't know how they were going to weather it.

Chapter 30

Mekhi walked out of St. Matthew's AME Church and sat down on the concrete steps leading to the main entrance. He placed his wool skully on his head, then blew into his hands. Rubbing them together, thereafter. He wanted to be alone. Too many people were inside. Many of them waiting and wanting a moment with his aunt.

The church had been filled to capacity during Desi's homegoing service. Everyone from students and staff of Arts High to the Mayors of Orange and Newark attended. It had all been a blur to Mekhi. His cousin had been carried to the church in a horse drawn glass-cased carriage. The family followed in matching limos. Streets had been blocked off to create a safe route for the horses to travel.

Indigo could barely walk down the aisle. She had to be assisted by Miguel and Stuff. Indigo let out shrieks of anguish throughout the ceremony, stirring the souls of everyone in attendance. She threw her head back and writhed uncontrollably in their pew. Mekhi watched his mother wrap her arms tightly around her, trying to keep what was left of her, together. She rested her head against hers and whispered things, unknown to him, in her ear.

Indigo and Maggie both, slipped in and out of

consciousness during the course of the service. The stewardesses stayed close with cups of water, tissue, and fans. They did their best to comfort the two women, but their angst was far too great for any consolation. Stuff sat in Miguel's embrace, crying quietly to himself. Mekhi had never seen either one of his uncles cry before and never wanted to see it again. The only person who maintained her composure was his mother. He sat in awe of what he thought was her strength. Little did he know she was simply numb.

He sniffled back a fresh set of tears as he closed his eyes and thought about his grandfather and Curtis . . . and Desi. Curtis's death had been declared a homicide and Desi's, a suicide. It made sense—Desi's departure, that is. She couldn't swim. In fact, she was terrified of any large body of water. So when the Medical Examiner confirmed that the act behind her death was deliberate, Mekhi, in particular, knew his cousin had gone inside of herself. So far down deep that no one could reach her. Not even him. She didn't want to be saved. Mekhi decided right then and there that after he graduated from St. Benedict's, he was going to go away to college. There was too much death here. And he didn't want to know this kind of pain anymore.

Ekua walked out of the church, immediately catching sight of him on the steps. She approached him cautiously, then sat down beside him. "Your mom is looking for you," she said in a hushed tone.

"Aiight." He sniffled.

She placed her hand gently on his back and began to rub it. "Is there anything I can do for you?"

Mekhi shook his head, trying to fight the urge to cry. He failed. He buried his head in his lap and sobbed long and hard.

Ekua wiped falling tears from her cheeks and laid her head on Mekhi's shoulder. She'd never lost a friend before. She'd never lost *anyone* before. She and Desi talked about *everything*. They talked about how much she loved Curtis. Ekua knew about the beating she received at the hands of her mother and how she was going to be forced to have an abortion. But Desi never led her to believe that she was going to kill herself. Ekua just wished her friend, her *best friend* had texted or called her before she jumped off that bridge. She might have been able to talk her down.

Karma emerged from the sanctuary, frantically searching for the two teenagers. She placed one hand on her hip and the other under her nose once she spotted them. They were the most pitiful things she'd ever seen.

Even though she'd met Ekua only a few weeks ago, Karma liked her very much. And she was happy the young woman and Mekhi had made amends. She was good to him. And, most importantly, good *for* him. Ekua had been spending a lot of time over to her house lately. The two were slowly getting to know each other. And what Karma could gather thus far, was that she had a good head on her shoulders. She was very driven. And she'd also been a big help to the family during Desi's disappearance. She'd passed out flyers, posted them on light poles and abandoned buildings, and created a student-based search team for her sister-friend. But what truly impressed Karma was Ekua's ability to comfort Mekhi during this tumultuous time. She was very present and patient with him.

Karma took in a deep breath before approaching them. She bent down and placed her hands on their arms. "Come on back inside, babies," she said, rubbing the nape of their necks with her thumbs. Ekua and Mekhi gradually stood to their feet. Just as Karma reached for their hands, she looked up and noticed Money standing across the street. He was watching her. Closely.

"Let's get you cleaned up." She looked back at Money.

He never blinked.

It had been a long and exhausting day. A stressful week. He kissed her sweetly on the temple before walking out of their bedroom and into the hall.

"She asleep?" Karma asked Stuff, as she placed the last of the dishes in the dishwasher. He had just finished tucking Indigo in for the night and peeked in on a deep sleeping Maggie.

"Yeah. They both are." He yawned. "Indigo needed to sleep. I'm just happy I didn't have to give her any sleeping pills to put her to rest. Her body shut down on its own." He rubbed the back of his neck as he settled down on one of the stools at the island in the kitchen.

"Good. You need to go on to bed yourself."

"I can't." Stuff locked eyes with her.

"You need to try," Karma insisted.

"I see ''im, Karm," Stuff admitted.

"Who?" Her brows furrowed.

"Curtis. "Dat lil' nigga's been hauntin' me since the day Desi was found. Every time I close my eyes, he's there. Smilin'. Like he won somethin'. Like he won her. Shit, sometimes I think I see 'im when I'm awake. Standin' in a corner or behind me. I can't go to sleep. And I don't wanna stay awake. It's my fault Desi's dead. I don't need anybody tellin' me dat. Indigo's goin' to blame the both of us for drivin' her away to a place where we couldn't save her. I know dat, too. I just don't know why this lil' nigga won't leave me alone."

"You killed him, Stuff," Karma replied in disbelief.

"So? He's not da first and he probably won't be da last."

"And with that being said . . . was it worth it? Was it worth losing your daughter?"

"No. Maybe . . . I don't fuckin' know!" He ran his tongue across his teeth. "I only wanted the best for dat girl."

"I know."

"I would have given her the world if I could," he said through angry tears.

"I know and so did she." Karma took his hands into hers. "What else is there to say other than . . . this is your cross to bear, just like Jimmy's mine," she said. "Look at me, Stuff."

He did as he was told.

"Carry it," she ordered.

Chapter 31

"Happy New Year!" the patrons of *Afro-Cubana* exclaimed.

Karma and Hassan stood in the middle of the crowd embraced in a passionate kiss. Marriage suited them well. They'd gone to the Justice of the Peace early yesterday morning with Mekhi, Mimi, her aunt, uncle, and cousin in attendance. New Year's Eve was Hassan's birthday, and he wanted nothing more than to marry her on his day. It had been three weeks since they'd buried their beloved Desiree. Karma consulted Indigo first, making sure she was comfortable with the decision. She didn't want her much needed "happily ever after" to send Indigo to a dark place. Nor did she want her to think that Desi's death was a thing of the past, because it wasn't. She thought about that child every day. Understanding Karma's need for totality, Indigo gave her, her blessing.

The DJ began to play the classic disco hit, "The Boss," by Diana Ross, sending the crowd into a frenzy. The couple began to sway from side to side. Karma opened her eyes and smiled. Hassan returned the gesture. She wrapped her arms around his neck and licked her lips. Hassan could feel his nature rising, and he wanted her to feel it too. So he placed his hand on the small of her back and pulled her close. Karma could feel his hardness through his slacks. She bit her bottom lip before giving him a small, suggestive smile. She slid her hands down his arms, finding his hands afterward. If she was what he wanted at that very moment, then Karma was going to give herself to him. So she led him out of the dancehall and upstairs to her office.

Within two minutes of partially undressing, Hassan licked the length of Karma's neck as he thrusted in and out of her. She rode him carefully from underneath as he cupped her firm behind with his massive hands. Hassan had always fantasized about making love to Karma in her office. There was something very exciting about the possibility of getting caught. And when the thought crossed his mind, Hassan remembered neither of them had locked the door. Karma opened her eyes and caught sight of a dark figure standing in the doorway. She couldn't make out the face. But when the person stepped out of the darkness, her heart skipped a beat.

"Money," she moaned.

Four minutes away, at the Robert Treat Hotel, Mekhi stood beside Carmine against a wall, watching Ekua grind against his throbbing penis. He smiled with pleasure as he grabbed her hips and began to grind back. The couple's favorite song, "Wild Thoughts," blared overhead. Mekhi was happy they'd been able to get back to some sort of normalcy. Hell, they were survivors and celebrating the

New Year *together*, as friends, as a couple, was the right thing to do.

Two guns, aimed and fired. At the same time, for the same reason. Pandemonium erupted. No one could distinguish the sound of a human wail and a police car siren.

They barely made it out alive. Carmine had seen Jamie first. By the time Mekhi looked up, Jamie had the 9-millimeter pointed at him. Carmine pushed Mekhi and Ekua to the floor just as the gangbanger pulled the trigger. Someone tried to slap the gun out of his hand, but he wouldn't release it. Shots rang out again, and Jamie fell aimlessly to the floor. Juan and the rest of the squad blended themselves in with the chaos, leaving their fallen brother behind.

The threesome pulled onto Ferry Street in a cab. Two ambulances, a fire truck, and too many police cars to count, lit up the entire block. The scene looked like something out of a movie. The street was blocked off with barricades, and Mekhi could see that most of the activity was happening outside of his mother's restaurant. He leaped out of the taxi and bolted down the street.

The restaurant was taped off. Two EMTs charged out of the front door, aggressively pumping air into the nose and mouth of someone on a stretcher. Mekhi recognized the face as that of Hassan's. He looked around frantically for his mother.

"Ma? Ma?" he called into the crowd of onlookers. He raised the caution tape and rushed the door, barreling through four police officers.

Mekhi ran through the cafe, past the bar and lounge, through the dining hall, where members of the staff and some partygoers were being questioned by police, to the hallway that led to the administrative offices. Two men dressed in trench coats and suits were standing outside of his mother's office deep in conversation. Flashes of light created silhouettes on the wall behind them. Mekhi's feet began to move beneath him. What started off as a slow drag turned into a full sprint.

"Ma? Ma?" he called, his voice bouncing off the walls. He captured the attention of the detectives.

They made an attempt to head him off at the path, but Mekhi sacked them, causing them all to crumple to the floor. Mekhi scampered to his feet and into the office. A heavyset woman, with "'CSI'" written on the back of her jacket, was hovering over, what looked like a body, on the floor. She had a sophisticated camera in her hand and snapped a photo. Then another. And then another. The shuttering of the flash sounded like thunder in Mekhi's ears. She remained for a moment, shaking her head at the sight before her. She took a deep breath in, then released it before moving to the side.

Mekhi's mouth fell open. "Oh nooo!" he hollered. "Nooo!" The photographer jumped, startled by his unannounced presence.

"You can't be in here," she said, moving toward him.

Pushing her out of the way, Mekhi sent her and her camera flying. He stood over his beloved mother. His blue eyes taking in the two large bullet holes that had burned through her dress. Her face was fixed in a cringe, as if she could still feel the fire from the bullets penetrating her chest and stomach.

"Mommy!" he screamed again, shaking uncontrollably. "Mommyyy!"

The two officers he'd bum-rushed outside charged into the room and grabbed him by the arms. Mekhi fought against them.

"Come on, son," one of them said, doing his best to get the hysterical young man out of the room without using brute force.

Mekhi, overwrought with anguish, lost feeling in his legs and collapsed in their arms. He continued to holler and cry for his mother all the way out of the building.

"He killed her!" He sobbed. "He fuckin' killed her!"

Mekhi's weight, that of his body and the loss of his mother, was too much for the detectives to carry. They were overcome with emotion and asked for the much needed assistance of the waiting medical technicians. Ekua and Carmine ran to Mekhi's side, wrapping their arms around him. There wasn't a dry eye in the crowd, amongst the police, fire, or ambulatory team. Mekhi was making each and every one of them think about their own mothers. *Forcing* them to treasure the life given to them *by their mothers.*

Chapter 32

"Right here," Mekhi said to the cab driver in a low, dark tone.

The cabby parked at the corner of Tremont and Berkeley Avenue. Mekhi took a twenty-dollar bill out of his coat pocket and handed it to the bearded man. He got out of the car and watched it speed off down the street. Once it turned the corner, Mekhi walked in the direction of Indigo and Stuff's house. It sat in the middle of Berkeley Avenue. He'd decided on the ride over that going home wasn't an option. He wasn't ready for the quiet. The police had contacted the rest of the family while he sat on the ground in front of his mother's business. He'd stopped cooperating with the police. He'd wanted to go back into the restaurant and sit with his mother, but they wouldn't let him. So he left. Ekua and Carmine tried to stop him, begging him to stay and wait for Indigo and Stuff to arrive. But their pleas fell upon deaf ears.

Mekhi walked up the driveway to the Victorian-style home with wild eyes. He surveyed the area, making sure no one was lurking in the shadows. He needed to get into the house. He figured his aunt and uncle were already down at the restaurant. Neither of their cars were there. Mekhi checked his pockets for something to pick the lock with. He came up empty-handed and began to look under a pile of rocks surrounding a bush near the door for the spare key. It wasn't amongst the shrubbery.

"Fuck!" Mekhi said.

Frustrated, he put his hand on the doorknob and turned it. The door was unlocked. Taken aback by his luck, Mekhi gently pushed the door open and entered the dark entryway. He closed the door behind him and climbed two stairs that led into the kitchen. He needed to get his hands on Stuff or Indigo's gun. They had to be somewhere in the house. But where?

Mekhi moved through the kitchen into the dining room. A large, round table sat in the middle of the room with a china closet settled against a wall in the corner. He looked to the left of him, where the foyer and living room were, then to the sun parlor on his right. Mekhi didn't know which room to search first.

"You're not gonna find 'em down here," Stuff professed in a steady tone. Mekhi snapped his body around, facing the direction from which his uncle's voice came.

Stuff was sitting on a worn loveseat set against a large window. An old record player rested on one side of it, a tower of records on the other. The piece of furniture had become his place of solace. He sat on that couch, in the same spot every night. Ever since Desiree's death.

Mekhi remained frozen in place.

"Ain't nothin' I can say to make you feel better. Ain't nothin' I can say to make you change ya mind about murkin' dat coward ass nigga. It's already made up. But if dere's anything I need you to understand, right now, in dis very moment . . . it's dat you're at war, nephew. Not only wit' ya'self, but ya history. You were born into dis shit. It ain't your fault. Dis shit right here all started wit' ya grandfather. Now, I don't know how much ya grandmother told you about 'im, but he was one cold-blooded muthafucka. He killed a lotta people. *A lot* of people. And ya mother's mother just happened to be one of 'em. She, like most of 'em, if not all of 'em, didn't deserve to die. She was . . . she was da most kind, compassionate, beautiful woman I eva had da honor of knowin' . . . of livin' wit.' She took my parentless ass in and loved me like her own. Ya aunt was a police officer around dat time, and ya father was her partner. He met ya mother at ya grandmother's birthday party. One thing led to anotha, and dey went out on a date. From what I was told, dey went to ya grandmother's house to visit wit' her and . . ." Stuff paused momentarily. "Ya mother found her upstairs in her room beaten to death. Ya parents spent a lot of time togetha afta dat and eventually fell in love. You were conceived. Ya mother almost lost her life bringin' you into dis world. But she held on an' fought so she could be around to see you grow. Some shit went down between ya father and his uncle. He told 'im some shit about himself dat he couldn't handle and da muthafucka took it out on you. Now, here we are. Da sins of ya grandparents were passed along to ya mother and father. Ya mother tried to break da cycle, but—" He stopped again. Thinking about Karma. "Your father is a dangerous muthafucka, Khi. More dangerous than *his* father. Why? Because he tried to take you out. His own flesh and blood." Stuff became quiet again. "There's a safe behind da Frank Morrison picture hanging above our bed. Da combination is Desi's birthdate."

Mekhi nodded graciously, his eyes bloodshot. Stone-faced. He turned away and began walking toward the foyer.

"Mekhi," Stuff called to his back.

Mekhi stopped, looking over his shoulder.

"He'll probably be walkin' along Central Ave. Look for him near the Dunkin Donuts in EO," he stated simply. "It ain't much light around dat area."

Chapter 33

Money took his hot cup of coffee out of the cashier's hand and walked out, stepping into the forbidding night. He clutched the collar of his wool trench coat, his shoulders hunched, and made his way down the deserted street. He turned onto Evergreen Place, a block away from the Dunkin Donuts and entered the Ramada Hotel. Money traveled to the concierge desk and waited to be assisted. He didn't notice Mekhi walking in afterward, then bypassing him to get to the lobby's bathroom where he stood behind the wall waiting and watching.

A petite Indian man emerged from a room across the lobby. He walked over, settled behind the desk, and smiled at Money.

"Good evening, sir," he said in a heavy Asian accent.

"Evening. I'd like a room, please. For one," Money expressed as he dug into his pocket for his wallet.

The attendant began to search the hotel database for a vacant rom.

"And how long will you be staying?" he asked innocently.

"Just for the night," Money admitted.

He'd already decided that he was going to leave, not only the state, but the country in the morning. Reports about Karma's death would surely be on every news station by daybreak. He had to disappear before then.

His intentions were to kill Hassan, not her. But when he saw them together, their bodies intertwined, Money snapped. Hearing Karma call out the name of the man he despised, drove him to a place of no return. She'd never said his name the way she said Hassan's when they made love. *Never.* So he pulled the sawed-off shotgun out of his coat, pointed it at them, and fired. He would never forget the look on her face when he stepped out of the darkness.

He escaped out the back of the building, throwing the gun into a sewer drain a couple of blocks away. Money hailed a cab and made his way to East Orange. He'd really messed up this time. Any plans he had to reconcile with Mekhi went right out the window.

"All right," the man said. "That'll be fifty dollars."

Money opened his wallet and took out a hundred dollar bill. He handed it to the concierge. "Keep the change."

"Thank you, sir." He smiled wide. "Here is your key. You're in room 417."

Money nodded and took the key from his hand. He made his way to the elevator, pressing the up arrow, and waited. When the elevator finally reached the ground level, Money hopped on. He pressed the number "4" button on the wall, then the "close door" button. Mekhi took the nearest stairwell.

The ride up was a smooth one. The heavy steel doors

opened and Money stepped out, sipping on his temperate beverage. He walked down a long, narrow hallway with walls that would probably tell what they'd seen if they could talk.

Money reached the door of his assigned room and inserted the key into the lock. A buzzing sound ensued, and he entered thereafter. He didn't realize he'd dropped the second room-key outside of the door. He searched the wall for a light switch, but couldn't find it. He cursed under his breath as he made his way over to the bed and turned the lamp on the nightstand on. He removed his coat and threw it over a chair sitting nearby, then his shoes. Money took another sip of his drink and exhaled the evening's events, spreading its germs into the stiff air. He decided he was going to take a shower. He was in dire need of cleansing, of washing his greatest sin away. So he unbuttoned his shirt, throwing it on top of his coat. Then, unzipping his pants and placing them on top of the shirt. He traveled to the bathroom, flicking the wall light on and turning on the shower. The sound of the water beating against the porcelain tub blended with Money's racing heart. Both were loud and consistent. He moved toward the toilet and urinated as the room began to fill with steam. Money closed his eyes in euphoria. He flushed the toilet thereafter and settled at the sink. He hung his head, shaking it in an attempt to remove the image of Hassan and Karma from his mind. He stood in a fog. The steam had created a heavy, white cloud around him. When he outstretched his arm and wiped the moisture from the mirror away, a pair of blue eyes were piercing back at him. And before Mekhi could take the safety off his gun, Money snatched his .45 off the sink and placed it against his temple. Then fired.

Mekhi, stunned, watched the man who'd given *and* taken his life, fall violently onto the floor. He slowly lowered his pistol, then bit down on his bottom lip. A habit of his mother's.

Epilogue

The distinguished Hampton University faculty and proud family members of the 2021 graduating class applauded the six-foot-five, one hundred and ninety-four pound valedictorian as he walked up to the podium. Donned in his black mortarboard and gown, with Honor cords and the Presidential Scholar Medal around his neck, Mekhi bowed his head and grinned bashfully. He never did like being the center of attention, but he possessed such a commanding presence now, as a man, that he could only embrace it with humility.

Mekhi had overcome insurmountable odds. Now as a motherless child, he had to celebrate this day of accomplishment, of national appreciation for mothers, without his own. His years at the illustrious HBCU had been the best years of his life. The lifelong friendships he'd created and leadership positions he'd held, like that of Student Leadership President, Chapter Vice-President of the National Society of Black Engineers, and secretary of the distinguished Alpha Phi Alpha fraternity (Gamma Iota Chapter) had shaped him into a living example of the university's "Standard of Excellence" platform.

The campus was built upon an old plantation. The souls of the black and Native American slaves still walked its grounds, but their presence never bothered Mekhi. He often sat and studied in the arms of Ekua, under the Emancipation Oak, the notable tree where President Lincoln freed the slaves. She too, had attended the university, excelling just as much as Mekhi in her studies, extracurricular activities, and peer relationships. There was nothing like walking the sacred grounds of that campus at night with her, and then sitting down on one of the benches at the waterfront and listening to its stillness. If one listened close enough, he could hear the faint voices of his ancestors singing against the ebb and flow of the tide.

Mekhi could feel the company of his ancestors in his room when he woke up that morning. His grandfather, grandmothers, cousin and mother were all there. They helped him to rise and get ready for the day. Wrapping their arms around him, laying of their hands, holding him so that he could stand. Not only on their strength, but in his unwavering faith in God.

He looked up and into the sea of brown and black faces, his crystal blue eyes clear and focused. Smiling once again.

"Good morning, President and First Lady Harvey, faculty, peers, and family. We are gathered here today to celebrate a feat that many of us thought was far out of our reach, and the women who bore us, reared us, cried for us, prayed for us . . . *believed* in us when we didn't believe in ourselves." He paused momentarily. "My mother, Karma Alonso-Turner was born to a little Afro-Cuban woman from Clifton Forge, Virginia and a broad-shouldered black man from Orange, New Jersey. She was an entrepreneur and philanthropist. He was a decorated Army vet. And they raised her in a city infamously known for its crime and poverty—Newark, New Jersey. My grandparents kept her safe in the arms of their home and my grandmother's restaurant. Instilling in her the importance of family, integrity, responsibility, resilience and God. She grew up, in that city, during a time where one could get shot and killed while walking down the street. And it was in those streets where she learned how to *survive*." Mekhi paused once again. "I lost my mother when I was seventeen- years-old. She was a victim of gun violence and died at the hands of my father. I'm sure you can imagine how difficult it is for me to stand before you today and speak of her in the past tense—on this day, in particular—Mother's Day. It is not something I ever dreamed. My mother . . . loved me with all of herself, with every fiber of her being. She loved me like she loved all of her family . . . *hard*. I was not the Mekhi I am today, back then. I was a lost boy who blamed her for my misery, for not having my father in my life, even though I knew he wasn't suited for fatherhood. She did her best as a *single, black, working* mother raising me. I had the best of everything. I never went without. But I spent the majority of my early teenage years in and out of juvenile detention centers. Worrying her to a point where she often questioned herself as a mother—as *my* mother. I eventually got myself together with the help of my family. My aunts, my uncles, my sister, my girlfriend, and my step-father, who are all here today."

The congregation applauded the family's efforts as Mekhi locked eyes with them. He could see Indigo blowing kisses at him and Hassan patting his wet face with a handkerchief.

"The first day of the new year will mark the fifth anniversary of her death. It is a day that will forever haunt me. People *dream* of having the kind of mother I was blessed to have. She was beautiful, she was intelligent, she was accomplished, she was kind . . . she was a gift. I would not be here today had it not been for the sacrifices she made."

Mekhi could feel his soul beginning to stir. Tears welled in his eyes as he tucked in his lips and tried to maintain his composure.

"Mommy, as I look toward the heavens for you, with tears falling from my eyes . . . I thank you for loving me without reservation. I thank you for moving mountains and settling troubled waters. Thank you giving me wings so that I could soar. Thank you for giving me time. Time to change for the better. Time to be the good son you so deserved. These last four years without you have been rough. Some days I find myself not being able to get out of bed. But then

I hear your voice in my ear saying, *'Mommy's here.'*

"I say to my peers, the graduating class of 2021, we are the reflections of our mothers. Whatever path you decide to take tomorrow, remember to walk it with grace and beauty, dignity, and fervor. Illuminate the world with your light." Mekhi looked toward the sky again and shook his head.

"Mommy, you can rest in peace now. I'm okay. I love you always . . . my candle in the wind." He nodded and stepped away from the lectern thereafter. The crowd erupted into thunderous applause. Mothers, great, grand, and God-appointed aunts and sisters, all were wiping tears from their eyes. They rose to their feet and celebrated the young man who had stumbled and fell, but rose, like the phoenix out of the ashes, in the end.

Karma 3: Beast of Burden
Reading Group Discussion Questions

1. Do you think Mekhi was wrong for leaving his grandfather for dead?

2. Who do you think is to blame for Mekhi's poor behavior?

3. Do you believe Karma deserved a second chance at love?

4. Do you think Karma was wrong for falling in love with Hassan?

5. Do you think Mimi should have told Money what was going on between Karma and Mekhi?

6. Do you think Miguel was right to blame Karma for the fight between Mekhi and Money?

7. Do you think Indigo and Stuff overreacted to the news of Desi's unchaste status?

8. Do you think Karma really wanted to commit suicide?

9. Why didn't she succeed at her attempt and Desi did?

10. Do you think Money's rage was a result of no self-control or mental illness?

NEW TITLES FROM WAHIDA CLARK PRESENTS

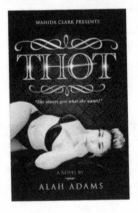

#READIT

WWW.WCLARKPUBLISHING.COM

CPSIA information can be obtained
at www.ICGtesting.com
Printed in the USA
BVHW08174209052 2
636553BV00001B/16